FIND HER

FIND HER

GINGER RENO

HOLIDAY HOUSE · NEW YORK

To our missing . . .
May they find their way home.

AUTHOR'S NOTE

Find Her is a work of fiction, but the Missing and Murdered Indigenous Women and Girls (MMIWG) epidemic, unfortunately, is not. Although I've tried my best to imagine, I don't believe any fictionalized story could adequately convey the real anguish these families must go through on a daily basis. If you have a missing loved one, my heart and my prayers go out to you.

Please be aware, in addition to the MMIWG epidemic, Wren's story also deals with instances of animal abuse.

Chapter One

The night sky drew Wren to the window. Her hand went to the turquoise pendant around her neck. She closed her eyes as she ran her fingers over the grooved stone and tried to remember…

She could almost see her—the same dark hair, dark eyes that stared back when Wren looked in the mirror. But it had been so long now. It was hard to make her mother's smile, her laugh, her touch, come into focus. So instead, Wren whispered a prayer into the darkness. As if somehow the winds might carry her words away and bring back the answer.

"Where are you?"

She sat down at her desk and stared at the screen of her laptop, deciding which site she should check next. But it was late, and she had school. She closed the lid and leaned back in her chair. Another day of hopeful searching done. Another day that had turned up empty. Wren was no closer to finding her answer than when the day had first begun. No closer to finding her mom. Missing: five years, three months, and twelve days. Disappeared without a trace.

But then, there was always tomorrow.

Chapter Two

Like everybody else in last period, Wren's eyes were glued to the front of the room. Mr. Pipkin, her second-favorite teacher of her least favorite subject, was explaining the finer points of percentages. Although a few in her class looked as if they might actually be paying attention, most were staring at the clock on the wall above Mr. Pipkin's head instead. Waiting for that magical moment when the final bell rang and they could break loose from the confines of Fort Gibson Middle School.

Wren folded her arms and leaned forward on her desk. School was okay, she guessed. She didn't hate it. But it did seem like they wasted a lot of time on things she would never need. The periodic table? War of 1812? Seriously? When is that *ever* going to come up in conversation? And don't even get her started on math. There's a perfectly good calculator on her phone.

Five more minutes.

She drummed her fingers.

Five minutes until the weekend. She glared at the second hand and could swear it went backward.

Her stomach growled. Lunch felt like days ago and she was starving. Elisi, her grandmother, was picking her up after school. They were meeting with some of her friends and going for burgers at Giggle Fish.

Wren chided herself. Not *her* friends. She didn't have any. Not really. When it came to Wren, almost everybody at school fell into one of three categories: 1) scared of her cop dad; 2) freaked by the whole missing mom thing; or 3) way too interested in both.

Okay, if she was honest, it was possible that she was a little to blame for her friendless state. It's not exactly like she put herself out there. All that bonding-with-another-human-being stuff was way too much work requiring way too much energy. Especially, when some days—on bad days—it was hard enough to get out of bed.

Besides, she liked spending time with Elisi and her friends. Who wouldn't want to hang with a room full of strong, brown-skinned women eager to share Cherokee ways and always had a story to tell?

If Wren was lucky, some of those stories would include memories of her mom. Glimpses of her mother's life that let Wren see her through others' eyes. Others she knew who loved and missed her mom too.

"*Remember when...*" one would say.

"*Or that time she...*" another might chime in.

But what Wren loved to hear most was, "*You remind me so much of your mother.*" Those were always accompanied by a warm, misty-eyed smile or a big hug.

Sometimes the group would cook, sometimes they'd bead, sometimes it was cards or dominoes. But regardless of the chosen activity of the day, there was always laughter. And laughter really can make you feel better about almost anything.

The sharp clang of the bell was followed by a collective sigh of relief that Mr. Pipkin seemed not to notice. He raised his voice to be heard over a room full of slamming textbooks, zipping backpacks, and chairs scraping across linoleum. "No homework, guys." He smiled as if giving himself a gift, too. "Have a good weekend. See you Monday."

Finally. She was free.

As soon as she cleared the main double doors, she saw Elisi in the parking lot, waving to get her attention. Wren chuckled, as if failing to notice Elisi, standing outside an old (Elisi would call vintage) turquoise-blue truck would ever be an option. She was a presence. As bright as the sun.

Wren tossed her backpack onto the seat and hopped in. "Hey!" She rubbed her hands together. "We still doing Giggle Fish? I'd kill for a cheeseburger basket."

Elisi's eyebrows shot up. "Hey? Is that any way to greet your grandmother?"

Wren leaned over and pecked her on the cheek. "Siyo," she said and gave her a sheepish smile. "Sorry, I don't know how to say 'cheeseburger' in Cherokee yet."

Elisi laughed. "Okay, okay, Giggle Fish it is. But first, we're stopping by the store. I've been thinking...you spend entirely too much time holed up in your room on that computer." She shot Wren a knowing glance. "Enough is enough. You may not want to hear it, Usdi, but you need something else to focus on. And I have an idea." With that, she pressed in the clutch and shifted into first gear.

Wren sighed. What Elisi meant was she needed to focus on something other than looking for clues about her mom.

She didn't know how, but Elisi always knew what she was up to.

☉⊘☉

Elisi pulled into the store's parking lot and shut off the truck. It had been a quiet ride. She turned toward Wren. "I want her found too, Usdi. Of course I do. But while she's gone, she'd want me to take care of you—make sure you're okay. And constantly having your face buried in that laptop looking for her isn't healthy. Your mom wouldn't want that."

Wren's chest tightened. Healthy or not, she had a routine, and it kept her sane. "B-b-but...the animal shelter...I'm helping Landry. I can go more often. I will. I promise." She nodded, eyes wide, frantic to make Elisi believe.

All the color must have gone from Wren's face, because Elisi suddenly looked worried. Her eyes teared. She laid a hand on Wren's shoulder. "I know you're trying to help, sweetie. I just hate watching what it's doing to you—what you're missing." She gave Wren a sly grin to lighten the mood. "I mean, seriously, your idea of fun is eating french fries with a bunch of old ladies?"

Elisi's smile softened. "I'm not saying you have to stop completely, hon. I'm just saying, you really need to spend some time on other things, too. Other normal, twelve-year-old things."

Wren blew out a slow breath. The kind when something turned out not as bad as what you had braced yourself for. That was something she was good at. Preparing herself for the worst. Like an invisible cloak of protection always at the ready.

Elisi's eyes, now dry, danced with excitement as if she was about to pitch the very best of ideas. "Usdi, you are so good at finding things and noticing what others miss." She shook her

5

head. "You amaze me. Why, you found a dog and two cats alone in the last three weeks."

Wren shrugged it away. "It was the same cat twice. Mr. Moody keeps leaving their garage door open." Now, it was Wren's eyes that lit up. "This last time, Booger got stuck up in that big oak tree—you know, the one over by the football field. Anyway, all I had to do was open a can of tuna, put it at the base of the tree, and sit and wait. Once he got hungry enough, he came right down."

"See, that's what I'm talking about. You're very good at this." She unbuckled herself and reached for her purse. "Now, what we're going to do is go into this store and pick out some paper. And then you're going to print up some flyers. You, my dear, are going to make your finding business official."

Wren nodded slowly, not anywhere near 100 percent sold, but Elisi seemed sure enough for the both of them. And when she got this way, Wren knew better than to protest.

Elisi already had one foot out the truck door but she stopped and turned back toward Wren. "Remember, Usdi, when we are hurting, the best thing we can do is help others. To give another joy, is to ease our own pain."

Chapter Three

FINDER OF LOST THINGS, shouted the big block letters on bright yellow paper. Wren had made enough flyers to hit most of the main spots by noon—library, post office, bakery, hardware store, McDonald's. It doesn't take long to cover the 13.4 square miles of Fort Gibson, Oklahoma, on a Saturday, even on a bike.

Each place she visited had a bulletin board with typical business-type notices: LICENSES, HOURS OF OPERATION, EMPLOYEE OF THE MONTH, that kind of thing, mixed with assorted tear-a-tabs for BABYSITTING, HOUSECLEANING, and TRUCKS FOR SALE. And at each place, she made sure to post her FINDER flyer in the prime-est vacant spot—even if those spots weren't exactly vacant when she got there.

The more she'd thought about it, Elisi was right. Wren *was* good at finding things for people. But her real talent, her real sweet spot, was missing pets. She couldn't explain it. Only that she had a nose for it. She'd get this feeling—what she secretly called a "finder feeling"—that would almost always help her to bring them home.

Her dad called it "cop-ley intuition." That gut feeling cops get when they're working a case. Whenever Elisi would brag that Wren had found another one, and gush about how thankful the owners were, Wren's dad would beam and say something like: "Keep it up and I'll have to give you a badge," or "We'll make an officer out of you yet!"

Wren would smile back and try to match his beaminess. Of course, she was happy he was proud, but her...an officer? Not exactly sure how she felt about that. She was proud of her father and what he did. And she had no doubt that if her mom had gone missing in his jurisdiction, things might have been different. But there was no arguing that, for some, missing cases of people who looked like her mother weren't a priority—even those married to a police chief. To Wren, "protect and serve" should apply to everybody. And the fact that it didn't, left a bad taste in her mouth.

She coasted up the driveway, dumped her bike in her yard, and burst through the front door. Elisi, as usual, was the only one there. Her dad, as usual, was at work.

She dropped her backpack on the kitchen floor and climbed onto a barstool. She leaned over and pulled out a leftover flyer from the front pocket, smoothed out the fold, and reviewed her handiwork. "So...Elisi...," she said, scrunching her brow, "why do you think I'm so good at finding things?"

Elisi bumped the oven door closed with her hip and plopped down a tray of Elisi's Famous Chocolate Chip Oatmeal Cookies on the counter between them, filling the house with the smell of warm sugary heaven. She pushed away a strand of gray hair with the back of her hand. "Don't be silly, Usdi. You are a natural-born tracker. That's from your Native half, for sure." She pulled a gallon of milk from the refrigerator door, poured Wren a tall glass, then nodded toward the white liquid. "As far as your other, much paler half helping you find anything?" She scoffed and held up her hand. "Columbus. That's all I'm saying."

Wren chuckled. "Elisi, I'm not a baby anymore. You don't have to call me Usdi."

Her grandmother waved her off. "You'll always be my Usdi. I'll always be your Elisi." She took a cookie for herself, slid the tray closer to Wren, and shrugged. "Live with it."

Wren grinned and reached for a cookie, slowly breaking it in two. The warm gooey chocolate stretched the gap and coated her fingers. Suddenly, she felt a familiar sting in her eyes. The same sting that happened whenever the feelings she kept shoved in the background came rushing up front. Wren shook her head. *Get it together. Don't let Elisi see,* she chided, instantly mad at herself that something so simple—so innocent as a cookie—could cause such a reaction. But it wasn't like she didn't know why. Elisi's Famous Chocolate Chip Oatmeals were their favorites. Wren and her mom.

Her throat closed. She hated these random times when it snuck up on her, taking her breath away like a punch in the gut. The unpredictable and cruel reminders that no matter how hard she tried, she couldn't fool herself. That just like the cookie she held in her hands, she was broken too.

Wren looked at Elisi, who was oblivious to what she had triggered. She was much too busy clearing the cookie-making mess and starting on dinner to see Wren swipe away the tear that trailed down her cheek.

She had to get out of there. Out of sight of Elisi. She shoved her cookie in a napkin, got up, and threw it into the trash. "Thanks...," she managed, grabbing her backpack. "Homework." Her voice cracked. And as fast as she could, she retreated. Down the hall, into her room, and closed the door.

Chapter Four

Monday, after dropping her backpack at home, Wren pedaled down Poplar Street and around to the east side of the single-story Town Hall building, to the main entrance marked POLICE. She leaned her bike against the wall, leaving her bike lock hanging loose. It was doubtful, at least in this town, that anyone would be crazy enough to steal from a cop's kid.

Inside the door and down the hallway, an officer walked out the security entrance. He reached back and caught the door before it closed so she wouldn't have to be buzzed in. "Hey, Little Mac," he said, using the short version of her last name. "How's it going?"

Big Mac, although nobody in their right mind would ever call him that, was Police Chief William P. MacIntosh. Most people in town called him Chief. She called him Dad.

"Hey, Dooley." She slipped under his outstretched arm and through the door. Wren liked Dooley, but she didn't bother to answer his question, figuring it was one of those things people ask that they really don't want to know. The door clicking shut behind her told her she'd figured right.

As she walked down the hallway toward her dad's office, past the desks and cubicle partitions they called the bullpen, she heard an officer call out.

"Chief's not here. He's in with the mayor."

She stepped back to see Officer Granger sitting at his desk. She lifted her hand. "Hey, Grange. Yeah, I know."

Granger sat his coffee mug down and leaned back. The leather and all the stuff on his duty belt groaned against his chair.

She glanced around. "Landry here?"

"Nah...was earlier but he got a call. Loose husky over off Walnut."

Wren scrunched her face. "Hmmm...probably Milo. The Jamisons live close to there. Maybe I should give them a call."

He tapped his pen against his other hand. "You know...as much as you help out at that shelter, you ought to be on the payroll."

"Yeah, right, tell my dad—" The desk phone rang.

Granger's face went all businesslike as he reached for the handset, excusing her with a quick wave of his other hand. "Officer Granger. How can I help?" he said as he tucked the phone under his chin and began typing on his keyboard.

What Granger—or her dad—didn't know was Wren always showed up early on purpose. Meetings with the mayor usually ran long, which gave her more than enough time to snoop. Her dad was old-school. He liked to print out hard copies of "be on the lookouts"—what cops called BOLOs—of wanted crooks in the area. And more importantly, to Wren anyway, alerts that included missing-person updates and notices of unidentified remains.

Unfortunately, her dad was also very much by the book, so sharing information with anybody not law enforcement was out of the question. Even if the information was about his own wife and that somebody was his own daughter.

It was hard sometimes. Trying to understand. Trying not to be angry at him—at the police in general. Trying to wrap her head around that he or the investigating officer in charge of her mother's case might know something but was choosing not to tell her. All because of some stupid oath and a badge. Keeping things from her, from Elisi, was cruel, even if it was for the sake of the investigation.

Sometimes the love she felt for her dad won the battle. Sometimes...sometimes the frustration would bubble up inside and spill over. Those were the times her love for him definitely lost.

"Wrenie," he tried to explain, "she disappeared outside my jurisdiction. There's a limit to what they'll share—even with me. Just like there's a limit to what I can share with you. I get frustrated too, but I can't blame them. It's protocol. Besides, any investigator worth their salt always considers the spouse a possible suspect."

This, more than anything, made her see red. Anyone who knew her mom, her dad, or ever saw them together knew that was ridiculous. Wren couldn't understand why that didn't make *him* mad.

To Wren, all that was more than enough justification for her snooping. Since her dad and the investigator wouldn't voluntarily divulge what they knew, her only choice was to get creative. To take matters into her own hands.

It wasn't hard to get to her dad's files. He kept them on top of the filing cabinet that, for her purposes, was perfectly situated away from the line-of-sight of the doorway. They stood, like little manila soldiers at attention, in one of those wire divider things that kept them separated and easy to grab—categorized, color coded, with the latest alerts in front of each folder. She couldn't help but roll her eyes every time she saw them. In addition to being an always-working, no-exceptions rule-follower, he just might be the official spokesperson for the everything-has-a-place-everything-in-its-place fraternal order.

She thumbed down the stack to MISSING PERSONS, and opened the file. Since she'd last checked, there were three new bulletins. She skimmed the basics: a man out of Tulsa, missing since August—credit card recently used at a convenience store in Oklahoma City; a ten-year-old girl taken by her biological dad, found unharmed—Wren had heard about that one on the news; and—her breath caught—UNIDENTIFIED REMAINS FOUND. The vise, always present around her heart and stomach, tightened as she scanned the page. It was a fine line Wren walked, between wanting to know—and being afraid to.

County: Cherokee.

Tighter.

Sex: Female.

Tighter.

Age: 50–65 years.

She sat down in her dad's big leather chair and blew out her breath. Not her mom. The vise returned to its normal setting.

Hearing her dad's voice down the hall, she scrambled to get the bulletins back in the file and the folder back in place. She slipped around the desk, plopped into the side chair, and stared down at her phone, pasting a bored look on her face for effect, just as he walked through the door.

He smiled at her as he laid a handful of paperwork on his desk, but not his real, full-on, glad-to-see-her smile. Something was up.

Her stomach knotted. Had somebody seen her? Had she been caught? Her eyes darted around the office. New security cameras she didn't know about?

"Hey, Wrenie," he said as he straightened the new stack of papers, so their edges were perfectly aligned. "Been waiting long?"

"Nah—" She relaxed...until she noticed the missing persons file had slipped through the wire divider and was sitting cock-eyed. Her mouth went dry as she tried to hide her panic. Now she was thankful for whatever he had on his mind. Otherwise, he would've spotted the tilted file the second he walked in. If he caught her, it's not like he would throw her in jail or anything, but unsupervised visits would no longer be allowed. His office and her information pipeline would dry up. She couldn't let that happen.

"B-but I'm starving. Can we go now?"

He laughed, "Okay, okay, just let me—"

She jumped up and grabbed his arm. "Come on...feed me now or be charged with first-degree child abuse."

He shook his head. "What—I don't know where—all right, all right. But it's my turn to choose and I choose Mexican." Knowing full well that was Wren's favorite.

"DONE! If we hurry, we can beat the rush."

He laughed again. "Unless everyone in town shows up at the same restaurant at the same time, I think we'll be fine."

He motioned her to go ahead of him and followed her down the hall.

"Oh crap!" She stopped short once they got to the security door. "My phone!"

She bolted back to the office, dashed around the desk, realigned the errant file, and was just about to the lobby when her dad walked back in, his phone pressed to his ear.

He placed his hand over his phone. "Sorry, Wrenie. Emergency. Rain check?"

"Sure." She nodded, not sure he waited long enough to hear her answer before brushing past her.

She hopped onto her bike as the sound of police sirens filled the air. The ear-shattering bellow of the fire engine's horn made her wince as it pulled from the station and rushed past her.

She thought about going back inside to see what was happening. Her dad wouldn't tell her, of course, but she wasn't above eavesdropping on Shelly in dispatch. Or even easier, she could sneak into an empty cubicle with a radio and just tune in. But frankly, she didn't really care enough to go to the trouble. There was only one case she was interested in, and this—whatever it was—wasn't it.

Chapter Five

"Morning," Wren grumbled as she flopped her backpack on the kitchen barstool beside her. The smell and sizzle of frying bacon was welcoming, but still, Wren hated mornings and getting ready for school. Especially this time of year. Theirs was a nice older home on the outskirts of town, but toward the end of the year, it could get drafty, requiring space heaters throughout to knock off the chill. Each winter, when the temperatures dropped, her dad toyed with the idea of moving them closer to the station—somewhere more "airtight"—but in the end, the vote was always to stay put. This house, with its gray siding and white trim. With a huge maple out front whose leaves flittered like pieces of silver in the Oklahoma winds, then turned into gold in the fall. This house was the last place any of them had seen her mom. So, the thought of moving felt too much like moving on.

The fall chill had moved in unseasonably early this year, so Wren was taking on the October day dressed in layers, in the highly likely event she would be forced to shed by midday. Forecasting the weather in Oklahoma and how to dress for it was always somewhat of a guessing game.

Elisi, busy in the kitchen as usual and full of early morning energy, threw open her arms. "Good morning, my dear Usdi!

How did you sleep? I am making you Elisi's Famous Pancakes and Bacon—the breakfast of champions." She set down a glass in front of her. "Want some juice?"

Wren smiled. "Yes, please." She took a drink when it was filled, then swiped her mouth with her sleeve.

Elisi cocked an eyebrow.

Wren gave her a sheepish smile and repeated the step with a napkin. She waited until Elisi turned back to the stove and stole a piece of bacon.

"Any calls?" She covered her mouth and tried not to sound like she was chewing. Her dad had insisted she use their home number on the flyer, not wanting Wren messing with this "finding business" on her phone during school. Which, by default, made Elisi her assistant.

Elisi pulled a slip of paper from under the tiger magnet on the fridge. A small effort on their part to show support for the school's mascot, and their designated leave-me-a-note spot. "As a matter of fact…" She slid the piece of paper toward Wren. "Susan Taylor. J.R. escaped again. Been gone a couple of days this time."

Wren's brow furrowed. It wasn't a job generated from one of the new flyers. Ms. Taylor, or Susan, as she insisted on being called, was already a repeat customer, and the one who had initially suggested Wren advertise as a way to earn some extra money. Wren had politely declined, never wanting to accept money for finding stuff—especially a lost pet. Taking money for finding a loved one just didn't feel right.

But then Elisi had encouraged her to do the same thing too. "It's no different than all those private-eye shows you watch on TV, Usdi, except they charge people just to look. You're only charging if you *find*." She nodded. "You're a much better deal."

Although the money thing still kinda made Wren's stomach hurt, she decided any cash she made could help support the animal shelter. As a volunteer, she knew firsthand they always needed something.

But...she also decided, for her stomach's sake, she wouldn't out-and-out charge a set fee. She'd only accept donations. She'd leave it up to the grateful clients to decide what her services were worth.

Wren picked up another piece of bacon, this time in plain sight. "Thanks, but don't have time for Famous Pancakes. And I'll go check on J.R. right after school."

ㅇㅇㅇ

J.R. was an eight-year-old Jack Russell terrier, who followed his nose wherever it took him. Even if that meant burrowing under his fence and venturing into Mr. Simpson's pasture, filled with short-tempered cows. He'd usually find his way home, but on occasion, he'd lose himself and Susan would ask Wren to find him. But he had never been gone this long before.

Susan opened her front door.

"Hi Ms.—Susan.... J.R. show up yet?"

Susan pushed open the screen. Eyes red. Her hair wrapped in a messy pile on her head. An oversized flannel shirt, gray sweats, white socks, and house shoes. She looked like she hadn't slept. Wren had her answer.

She stepped inside. "Let me get his blanket."

Susan chewed her thumbnail and shook her head. "He's been gone so long, Wren. Two days. I'm worried."

Wren walked over to J.R.'s corner and gathered up his blanket—baby-blue fleece with multicolored little paw prints—and headed back toward the door. "Don't worry," she teased to try to lighten things. "He probably just made a new friend and decided to sleep over." She shook her head. "Kids…they never call." Her joke had made Susan smile, but in truth, Wren was a little worried too.

Wren forced a smile. "It'll be okay, you'll see."

Susan touched Wren's arm at the door. "Please…I don't know what I'd do without him. He's my family." She drew back her hand as if realizing who she'd just said that to. "I'm-m sorry." She shook her head. "I wasn't thinking…"

Wren, having heard a lot worse from others that had been intentional, brushed it off. "It's okay. Really. I get it. Family is family." She started out the door, then stepped back. "You know, his blanket is usually enough. He's drawn back to his own scent. But I'm sure he's really missing you. I bet it would help to have something that smells like you, too."

In a flash Susan stripped down to her tank top and shoved the flannel shirt into Wren's arms. "I've had this on since he's been gone." She gave Wren a weak grin. "Trust me, it smells very much like me."

Wren chuckled. "It's perfect." She gave Susan her best reassuring smile. "Don't worry, I'll find him."

And then she said the two words no good PI—detective—cop—let alone a twelve-year-old amateur finder, should ever say: "I promise."

Chapter Six

Wren shivered at the chill in the air and zipped up her hoodie. From Susan's house, she rode straight over to the far side of Mr. Simpson's pasture. She spread out J.R.'s blanket and Susan's flannel shirt at the base of an old rotted-out oak tree at the highest point on the property, securing them with rocks she found close by so the north wind wouldn't whisk them away.

"This should work," she said as she stood and brushed the dirt from the knees of her jeans and her hands. "Okay, J.R., time to put that snoot of yours to use."

She looked around in all directions. Waited. Looked around some more. Nothing. No little brown-and-white dog bounding toward her, jumping into her lap giving what-took-you-so-long-to-find-me kisses.

She sat back down by the shirt and blanket. It wasn't like J.R. to stay out one night—let alone more. A gnawing in her gut told her something was wrong. *Really* wrong.

She scanned the area again. J.R. usually stayed around here, but if he wandered too far from home, he could lose his bearings. Wren knew—thank you, Internet—that planting something outside, like a blanket or bed with a familiar scent, can give their super-noses a little help in finding their way home. It had often worked for her in the past. That, along with her finder feelings telling her she was on the right track.

But this time, as she watched and waited and tried to will herself to feel more of that gut instinct stuff, she felt nothing. An uneasy nothing that told her she had to do something.

Landry.

Maybe Landry could help. She ran back to her bike, pulled her phone from her backpack, and called the shelter. Voicemail. *Rats.* She shot him a text too, but when he didn't answer right away, she jumped onto her bike and started crisscrossing streets. She might spot J.R.—or catch Landry out on patrol. Maybe, if she was lucky, Landry had already picked him up.

She asked around at the Dollar General and rode through both mobile home parks before having the bright idea to check out Mac's Drive-Inn. J.R. had to be hungry, right? She 100 percent expected to pull up and find him begging for french fries in the parking lot. But no…he wasn't there either. Her finder feeling had struck out. She shoved her hands into her jacket pockets and grimaced. *Okay, so, it's not a perfect science.*

There was nothing else she could think to do but go back to the pasture.

The cold air clawed at her lungs as she pumped the pedals hard. Her nose started to run. The closer she got to the tree in the pasture, she thought she could see something on the flannel shirt. But…her breath caught…whatever it was wasn't moving.

She dumped her bike on the grass and ran as fast as she could toward the tree and dropped to her knees. It was J.R. And he was bleeding. Badly.

Frantic, she laid her hand on his side and felt his shallow

breaths. Thank God, he was alive, but she didn't know for how much longer.

She dialed Elisi and almost screamed into the phone. "Grandma, J.R.'s hurt! I'm at Old Man Simpson's pasture. I've got to get him to Doc Foley's."

She hung up, not waiting for an answer. She knew Elisi would come. There was so…so much blood. It looked like it was oozing from his back leg, but she couldn't be sure. She tied Susan's shirt tightly around his lower body, hoping to slow the flow. She wrapped his blanket around him and scooped him up in her arms, pressing his body against her for extra pressure. Riding with him was out of the question. She ran as fast as she could. By the time she got to the corner of Fox Lane, Elisi was waiting, passenger door open. She hit the gas the second Wren's butt hit the seat. No one could ever say her Elisi drove like a grandma.

The truck tires spit gravel as they flew into the clinic parking lot. Elisi squealed to a stop right outside the entrance. She reached across Wren, jerked up the handle, and shoved open the door. "Go! I'll be right in."

Wren burst through Doc Foley's door. "HELP!"

Startled, a vet tech up front rushed over and took J.R. out of Wren's bloody hands. "What happened?" she asked while trying to visually answer her own question.

Wren, crying, shook her head, her blood-stained palms upward as if still holding him. "I—I don't know. He was lost. I just found him like this. He's bleeding. Bad. PLEASE! HELP HIM!"

The tech's face was full of concern, but she still managed a reassuring smile. "Have a seat, hon. Let me take him back and see what's going on."

Wren wiped the red from her hands on J.R.'s already-so-bloody blanket and plopped down in the nearest waiting room chair.

She could feel the receptionist and other pet-moms and -dads watching her with sympathy-filled eyes. Her head stayed down, her eyes glued to the floor. She'd gotten a lot of those looks in the last five-plus years. She hated them more than anything. Like they weren't seeing her when they looked—only her so-sad situation. Her stomach churned. The bacon from this morning's breakfast threatened to revolt.

She blew out long, slow breaths through her mouth until her stomach settled.

Whatever had happened to J.R. wasn't her fault, she knew that. So why did she feel so guilty? She had promised Susan she would find him, and, she had done that...but not this way. Not hurt. Not, God forbid, *dying*.

Elisi had parked the truck and rushed in. "What did they say?"

Wren, eyes wide, shrugged.

Elisi nodded and gave Wren a quick hug. "We need to let Susan know. Do you want me to speak with her?"

With everything inside her, Wren wanted to say yes. But finding J.R. had been her responsibility. So that meant this was her responsibility too.

She shook her head. It was easy knocking on an owner's door with their missing puppy or kitten in her arms. But this... she'd never had to do anything like this before.

She fished her phone from her back pocket.

Elisi touched her arm and gently let her know this wasn't something that should be sent in a text.

Wren nodded and blew out a breath. She could barely feel

her hands as she raised her phone to her ear. When Susan answered, Wren didn't waste any time. "Ms. Taylor, this is Wren." Her voice sounded so strained, she didn't recognize herself. "I'm at Doc Foley's, I've found J.R. Come quick."

It seemed like she had just hung up the phone when Susan threw open the entrance door so hard, it hit the wall behind it. She rushed to the reception desk. "J.R.—the Jack Russell that was just brought in. What's happening? How is he?"

The receptionist quickly got up. "Let me see what I can find out."

Wren stood as soon as she saw Susan and rushed over to the desk.

Susan's jaw dropped and her eyes flew open wide. "Oh my heavens—Wren—are you hurt too?"

Wren glanced down at herself and shook her head. Tears welled in her eyes. "It's J.R.'s," she cried. She dropped her head as she handed Susan J.R.'s bloodied blanket. "I'm sorry. I'm so, so sorry."

Susan gently led Wren back to her seat and sat down beside her. "What hap—"

"Susan?" Doc Foley came from the back, wiping his hands with a towel.

Wren and Susan stood, but couldn't make their feet move in his direction.

Doc Foley crossed over to them, put his hand on Susan's arm, and gave them both a comforting smile. "J.R. is stable for now. I'm afraid he's been shot."

"Shot?!" Susan repeated as if she surely hadn't heard right. Her knees buckled. He reached out, grabbed her arm, and guided her back down into the chair.

Wren's jaw dropped. She'd figured one of Mr. Simpson's cows had finally had enough of J.R.'s shenanigans and chased him until he'd caught himself on a section of the barbed wire fence. But shot? Who would do such a horrible thing?

"With your permission, he's going to need surgery. I need to get in there and see how much damage has been done." Doc Foley paused. "We'll do everything we can to save his leg, but of course, saving his life is our first priority."

Susan nodded, clearly in shock, struggled to get out her words. "Please... whatever it takes."

Doc Foley put his hand on Susan's shoulder. "Good. Good." He nodded. "I think it's best to wait until morning though. I'll pump him full of fluids and antibiotics overnight, so he'll be as strong as possible for surgery. Go on home now. I'll call you tomorrow." He gave the three of them a sympathetic smile. "Try not to worry.... He's in good hands."

They sat in silence until Elisi, who was sitting on the other side of Susan, touched her shoulder. "Susan, perhaps it's best you don't drive. May we take you?"

Susan shook her head. "No. Thank you. I'll be fine. I want to stay for a bit. Maybe they'll let me see him, so he won't be scared."

Elisi motioned toward the bloody blanket. "May I? I'd like to take it and say a prayer for J.R."

Susan's eyes filled with watery gratitude. "Yes...oh yes, please," she said, grasping Elisi's hand. "Thank you."

Elisi held on to Susan's hand for a moment, then turned to the vet tech. "May we have a bag for this please?" She slid the blanket gently inside the sleeve of clear plastic. She gave Susan one more comforting smile, then motioned to Wren. "Come, Usdi, it's time to go."

The drive back to the pasture to pick up her bike was silent. The bloody blanket, between them on the seat. Now more red than baby blue. Wren couldn't take her eyes off it. Couldn't believe what had happened. Couldn't wrap her head around anyone hurting J.R.—or any animal, on purpose.

She shook her head. This was no accident. No errant shot by a hunter. Nobody mistakes a two-foot terrier for a six-point buck. Besides, hunting or doing anything near Mr. Simpson's pasture was illegal. KEEP OUT and NO TRESPASSING signs were everywhere.

Anger began to burn deep in her belly, rising up, and setting her jaw. No, this was not an accident. It was flat-out meanness. Whoever did this was evil.

Whoever did this just wanted to kill.

Chapter Seven

Dinner that night was somber, even though her dad had actually made it home in time to join them. Elisi had made one of Wren's favorites. Elisi's Famous Tomato Basil Soup and Grilled Three-Cheese Sandwiches, made with thick buttered slices of Texas toast, cut at an angle. Wren liked to pour a spoonful of soup on the end of the sandwich, just big enough for a bite. Her very neat and orderly dad alternated soup, sandwich, soup. Elisi, she was more of a dipper.

But Wren was too worried about J.R. to enjoy her dinner. She dropped her sandwich on her plate and sighed. "Dad, are you listening? What are you going to do to find out who shot J.R.?"

Her dad put down his spoon, and dabbed his mouth with his napkin. "Has J.R.'s owner—Susan, is it? Filed a report?"

Wren just looked at him.

"You know I can't do anything without a report. Have her come down—"

Wren slammed her hands on the table. "She can't come down. Don't you get it? She's busy waiting to see if Doc Foley can keep him alive. That's way more important than your stupid piece of paper."

Elisi touched Wren's arm.

Wren pulled it away and stared into her tomato soup that, at this moment, looked a little too much like a bowl of blood.

Her dad's hand slipped under his glasses, and he squeezed the bridge of his nose. He blew out a slow breath. "I've got to have a report, Wren. There's nothing I can do about that. Have her call and I'll send Landry out to her. Either her house or Doc Foley's, all right? We'll try our best to look into it, but, Wrenie, there's a lot going on right now I can't speak to. And crimes against people come first. I'll—"

On the table, his phone vibrated against his glass of iced tea. He grabbed it and glanced down at the screen. His brow furrowed. He folded his napkin and placed it neatly beside his soup bowl and spoon, straightening his sandwich plate so everything was perfectly aligned. "I'm sorry." His chair scraped across the wood floor as he stood. "I've got to go back to the station."

He kissed the top of Wren's head. "I'll be back as soon as I can." He nodded at Elisi. "Thank you for dinner, Elisi. Delicious, as always."

Elisi gave him a nod that said, *You are welcome.*

And just like that, he was gone. Again.

Wren cleared the table, dumped the rest of her soup into the sink, and put the bowls, plates, and spoons into the dishwasher. She trudged to her room, flung herself onto the bed, and stared at the ceiling. She chewed on her lip and felt guilty. She should've apologized to her dad before he left. It was a house rule. Take care with your last words.

She wrapped her arms around one of her pillows. *Last words.* She couldn't remember her last words to her mother, no matter how hard she tried. It was too long ago, and Wren had been so young. She remembered days when she had been awful over something as stupid as dinner, or bedtime, or what she didn't want to wear, but she couldn't connect them to that exact day. Now, all those arguments seemed so silly. She wished like anything she could forget them. But no…guess things you're ashamed of are permanently ingrained, which hardly seemed fair. Especially when the one thing she wished she could remember, wished more than anything, continued to be elusive. *Did I tell her I loved her?*

She knew she hadn't said that to her dad.

She huffed and slapped her hands on the bed. But forgive and forget wasn't always so easy. Besides, she shouldn't have to apologize for something that was his fault. He could've helped her if he wanted to. Could've made an exception. But instead, he was constantly leaving. Constantly helping strangers. Constantly following pointless rules that made things so hard. Rules about J.R. Rules about her mom. Rules that left her and Elisi in the dark.

No. She sighed. If she owed anybody an apology, it was Elisi. It was a crime to throw away anything that came out of her kitchen.

She smiled at the thought and her anger faded. For as long as she could remember, every concoction Elisi made, no matter how simple, was referred to as Elisi's Famous "fill in the blank." Elisi's Famous Scrambled Eggs, Elisi's Famous Pop-Tarts, Elisi's Famous Toast. And, if you wanted something specific, that's exactly how you had to ask for it. By its full name, or it was a no-go. She knew it was just Elisi being goofy, but Wren loved every minute of it.

She got up to do what she should've done already. Apologize

and say thank you for her uneaten dinner—For Elisi's Famous Tomato Basil Soup from a can.

The second Wren opened her bedroom door, she smelled smoke. But she wasn't alarmed, recognizing the familiar sweet woodsy smell as it crept down the hallway. She followed her nose into the dining room, where Elisi was sitting at the table, eyes closed, saying a prayer in Cherokee, with J.R.'s blanket in front of her.

Wren watched in quiet reverence as Elisi moved her hands in slow, flowing circles. Mixing the cedar smoke that curled from the bowl beside her with her prayerful words. Wren's Cherokee wasn't anywhere near as good as it should be, and she couldn't understand all Elisi was saying, but she knew enough to know her grandma was calling forth healing spirits for J.R. Wren's heart swelled with gratitude. And even though she couldn't say the words, she closed her eyes in agreement.

"Ah, Usdi," her grandmother said, causing Wren to open her eyes. "I'm glad you took part. All will be well with your friend J.R."

Wren gave her a tentative smile. "I sure hope so."

Elisi shook her head and held up her finger. "No hope. It is done. Believe it."

Elisi got up from her chair and waved her hand back and forth as if shooing a bothersome fly. "Now, help me clear this smoke before your father gets home. Last time I told him it was a new air freshener." She chuckled. "But I don't think he bought it."

Wren laughed. It was no secret her dad wasn't exactly comfortable with all things Cherokee, but he didn't push back too much. Probably because he knew that without Elisi agreeing to leave her home in Tahlequah to help them, he would've been big-time sunk.

Wren opened the door and a few windows to help the effort, but it didn't take long for the outside to bring its chill inside the house, making them both grab for a sweater. They shut everything back up and cranked the space heaters.

Elisi lit a three-wick candle on the kitchen counter. "Pumpkin spice...that'll cover up anything." She chuckled again. "I'm sure your dad will love it."

Wren hugged her. "Sorry I was so grumpy."

Elisi patted her. "Understandable. When someone we care about is hurting, we hurt too. And sometimes that comes out as grumpiness. But, Usdi, it is important that we not take our pain out on others. Misery may love company, but there is no honor in making others feel bad just because we do. No honor at all."

Wren's eyes dropped to the floor. "I understand."

Elisi gave her another gentle squeeze. "Go on now. Get to bed. It's been a long day and school comes early. Tomorrow we will receive good news about your friend." She kissed her fingertips and turned her hand toward Wren. "See you soon, my sweet Usdi."

Wren did the same. "See you soon."

She switched off her bedside lamp, got settled, and tried her best to go to sleep. Instead she tossed and turned, twisting herself up in her covers, thinking of poor J.R. Unable to get the images, the metallic smell of blood on her shirt, on her hands, out of her mind. She'd scrubbed herself raw when they first got home, but the stench had taken up permanent residence in her nostrils.

oØo

"Remember, class." Mr. Dawson, Wren's social studies teacher, used his middle finger to push his clear-framed glasses up his nose. Considering everyone knew Mr. Dawson was more interested in his duties as assistant football coach than teaching seventh graders to be civic minded, Wren suspected there was probably something more to the gesture. "Test on chapter eighteen tomorrow." He sighed. "Will count for forty percent of your final grade." Now it was Wren's turn to sigh. Pretty much everything in Mr. Dawson's class was worth forty percent of their grade. Guess she should be thankful she had Mr. Pipkin for math class.

She had been so preoccupied with all things J.R., she hadn't so much as cracked open her books, let alone study a whole chapter's worth. Her luck, Dawson was serious this time about that 40 percent. If she tanked this test, her dad might shut down her finder business, ban her from helping at the shelter, and maybe even ground her. As far as he was concerned, anything that interfered with schoolwork should be illegal.

She chewed on her bottom lip. Not sure what she was going to do, other than wishing her finder feelings could also be used to find the answers to a test. No...her only hope was that she also had a gift for cramming a maximum amount of useless information, aka social studies, into her brain in a minimum amount of time.

But she'd worry about that later. Right now, all she cared about was getting an update on J.R.

C'mon, ring! She tried to coax the end-of-day bell. But she didn't have a gift for that, either.

She jammed her things into her backpack, slid her feet into a ready-to-sprint position. When the bell finally did ring, she bypassed her locker, grabbed her bike, raced home, and threw open the front door. "Any news?"

Elisi shuffled from her bedroom, wrapping her thick tan sweater tighter against the drafty chill. She looked different. Tired.

It caught Wren off guard, as if somebody had stolen her Elisi away and replaced her with someone...old. A jolt of fear coursed through her. She'd never once allowed herself to think of Elisi as aging. She was an elder, of course, Wren knew that. But she saw her as strong. Vibrant. Full of humor and color. Always. And Wren needed her to stay that way...needed Elisi to be in her life forever. No leaving allowed.

"My heavens," Elisi said, smoothing her hair, "is it that time already? I must have drifted off in my chair." She headed toward the kitchen. "Here, let me get you a snack."

Wren shook her head, deleting such scary thoughts. Denial was something she was much more comfortable with. "Have you heard from Susan? Anything about J.R.?"

Elisi covered a yawn with her hand, then waved her off. "I told you last night it was taken care of. Susan called and his surgery went just fine."

"And his leg?"

"Yes. Yes. He will be keeping all four of them."

Wren rushed over and threw her arms around Elisi.

Elisi hugged Wren back. "Silly girl," she said. "When will you learn never to doubt me?" She chuckled. "Now, are you hungry or not?"

Wren held on to Elisi's arm and laid her head on her shoulder. "How about we forget the snack and I make us dinner to celebrate?"

"You? Cook?" Elisi clasped her chest. "My...heart...can't... take...it," she said as she stumbled into the living room and collapsed on the sofa.

Wren plopped down beside her and made a fake scowly face. "HA. HA." Then she grinned. "And by make…" She held up her phone. "I mean make a phone call. How about a Wren's Most-Famous Hamburger and Tomato Pan Pizza?"

Elisi held up a finger. "With a side of Elisi's Famous Dr Pepper—make it a two-liter."

They laughed, and Wren reached over and gave her grandmother a hug. "Oh, Elisi, what would I ever do without you?"

Elisi patted Wren's arm. "Oh, Usdi, that's an easy one. You would turn white."

Chapter Eight

One way Elisi made sure Wren never turned all white was their trips to Tahlequah, the center of the Cherokee Nation. Tahlequah was Elisi's true home, born and raised, and the location of the Cherokee Marshal's Service. Since her dad worked with and had friends at CMS, the whole family sometimes went. But once every fall, Elisi and Wren made a special trip, just the two of them, to the Cherokee National History Museum.

Years ago, before her disappearance, Wren's mom and Elisi served on a committee to help turn the original Cherokee National Capitol Building into the beautiful, two-story, red-bricked building filled with Cherokee history that it is today. It was her mom's unrealized dream to work there once completed. Her dream to help others learn and remember.

On their way there, Elisi retold the story, as if Wren hadn't heard it before. Elisi squinted a little, like it helped her recall the memory. "After…" She trailed off, as if not wanting to say the rest of that out loud. She cleared her throat. "We were about through with the project, I think." She took one hand from the steering wheel and waved off the thought. "Actually, I'm not sure when exactly. It doesn't matter. Anyway, a formal photograph of the committee was commissioned to display at the opening—you know, one of those stuffy, get all dressed up, turn to the side and smile—in gratitude for our efforts. But unbeknownst to me, the rest of the committee had insisted they use an older, casual shot, snapped one day that captured our work in progress. There we were, sitting around the table, most of us in T-shirts and sweats, with books, plans, sketches, and coffee cups all over the place. We were so intent on what we were doing." She chuckled. "It was the furthest thing from professional, but they had insisted." Elisi choked up, then swallowed hard. "Because your mom was in the picture."

She turned toward Wren with watery eyes. "That meant so much to me.

"After the opening, each of the committee members got their own copy. Something to hold on to until she comes home, they'd said."

To believe together there will be good news, Wren thought.

So, each year, they had this tradition. Early lunch at Sam and Ella's, then the museum. First thing out of the car, they would stroll along the walkway made with rows of engraved bricks, until they came to the one with her mother's name. Elisi's knees not being what they used to be, Wren would bend down and slowly trace each letter with her finger, then stand and do the same over Elisi's open hand.

Maybe it was just Wren's hopeful imagination, but each time, something stirred in the center of her chest. Judging by Elisi's closed eyes and the look on her face, Wren had no doubt Elisi felt it too. That in that moment, as they walked through the museum doors, there were three of them.

Once inside, Wren went straight to the counter and grabbed an iPad for the interactive tour. She'd slip the strap over her neck and commence searching for new codes to scan. There always seemed to be something she hadn't seen before.

Elisi followed behind her, available for Wren's many questions, but mostly searching the nooks and crannies for memories.

They climbed the stairs slowly, taking the time to appreciate the artistry of the Origins Exhibit. A creation story brought to life. If possible, each time, Wren was more fascinated.

At the top, they would first go through the showcase of the seven clans. Elisi would hold her hand over a plaque and quiz Wren on a clan's trait. They played this game each year. "Repetition equals retention," she'd say. "Long Hair Clan?"

"Peaceful."

Elisi nodded, then would go to another plaque and switch it up. "Medicine?"

"Easy. Paint Clan."

"Bird Clan?"

Wren wadded her face to help access her brain. "Um…messengers?" Her answer sounded more like a question. Then she nodded. "Yeah, yeah…divine messengers between heaven and earth."

Elisi clapped her hands, then moved to the next plaque. She cocked her eyebrow in a you'd-better-know-this-one-or-you're-walking-home way and put her hand on her chest. "And we are…?"

Wren scoffed. "Duh…Wolf Clan!" She put her fists on her hips, struck a superhero pose, and said in her best superhero voice, "We. Are. Protectors!"

She then proceeded to ace the Deer, Blue, and Wild Potato Clans, without Elisi even having to ask.

Then it was on to try their hand at weaving a double-wall basket and where, every year, they would laugh, remembering the lopsided basket her mom had brought home from a class. Even with the step-by-step instructions, if her mom would've had the chance to try again, they were sure it would've still been hopeless.

And every year Wren's heart would break as they walked through the Trail of Tears Gallery. Tracing the long winding paths on the wall-sized map with her fingers. Reading of the cruelties her ancestors endured. Hearing the Cherokee voices all around her.

It was never an easy thing to see—to hear—to think about. Her stomach would churn. No matter how many times they came, she just couldn't numb or prepare herself enough to face that people could treat others that way.

But Elisi would remind her that they should also be inspired. Impressed with what the Cherokee had overcome. To know that the same blood that coursed through those survivors' veins now surged inside them, too.

It was a truth that always made Wren stand taller. And although there were a lot of things about her mother that seemed hazy the more time passed, one thing she knew her mom would've said at this moment was: *Warrior is in our DNA.*

All done, they sat on one of the benches, giving Elisi a much-needed rest. Both reflecting on what might have been. Her mom at the front desk, walking through the exhibits, smiling, and sharing her knowledge—just *not* making baskets.

Wren caught a glimpse of Elisi discreetly dabbing a tear, and it was a gut punch. Wren wrapped an arm around her and rested her head on her grandmother's shoulder. They sat there in silence. It was always a hard day for both of them, but it was also always one of the best. At first, the flurries of whats and whys would swirl around them, settling over their heads, weighing their hearts down like a wet soggy blanket.

What could've been. What should've been. What isn't.

Why her?

But then, for some unknown reason, things would just turn around. And suddenly, Wren would start to feel better. Was it her mom's spirit? She didn't know. Even though her mom didn't get to see it finished, maybe just being there, getting caught up in the energy of a place that meant so much to her, somehow, made Wren feel like she could still use the word YET.

That one day, someday, they *would* walk through these doors together.

The three of them.

And Wren wouldn't trade that feeling for anything.

Chapter Nine

The following Saturday, Wren planned to go to the shelter. She also planned to go early, but that's a plan that never really works out. Warrior may be in her DNA, but so was sleeping late on the weekends.

"Hey, Landry." Wren's bicycle brakes squealed as she pulled up next to his white truck with FORT GIBSON ANIMAL CONTROL on the door. Landry was Wren's favorite officer on her dad's force, by far. Not only was he an all-around good guy, he was solely responsible for the shelter's operation, which meant, unlike her dad, for Landry crimes against animals came first.

"Hey, kiddo." He smiled, unloading bags of food from the back of the truck. "Didn't expect to see you today." He nodded toward the bags. "Donation pickup. Nice, huh?"

He grabbed his gear out of the truck and escorted her inside the tan concrete block building that was his work home.

Once inside the door, Wren slipped off her backpack and pulled out a square plastic container. "Elisi's Famous Brownies right out of the oven." She waggled the container, enticing him, as if that was even needed. "Since you're so awesome, I thought you deserved some."

Landry smiled with his big blue eyes, military hair, and perfect teeth, and snatched the container out of her hand, tucking it under his arm like he was protecting a football. "You're right, I am awesome. And I do deserve them. But awesome doesn't mean I share."

She chuckled and followed him into his office.

Landry placed the container on his desk like he was handling squares of pure gold. Elisi's brownies were really that good. He plopped down in his chair. Those same blue eyes narrowed. "Wait a minute...." He leaned back in his chair. "Is this some kind of bribe?" He folded his arms across his massive chest. "Let me guess, you don't want to clean the kennels."

"Well . . ." She took the lid off the container. One long whiff of that warm gooey goodness with a dusting of powdered sugar was all it took.

He held up both hands in surrender "Okay, okay, fine. You've officially bought me off. No kennel duty."

Wren laughed. "Nah, I don't mind. I'll clean them. But...I do have a friend who can use some help."

Landry grabbed a brownie and swung his feet up onto the edge of his desk. "I'm all ears."

Wren sat down across from him and spilled her guts. J.R. getting shot, Doc Foley, Susan, her dad.

Landry lowered his feet off his desk, dropped the brownie remnant back into the container, and cleared his throat. "Wren, that's terrible. I'm sorry about J.R. and your friend." He shook his head. "But your dad's right. We can't do anything without a report." He grabbed a paper towel from the table behind him, swiped it across his mouth, and winked. "How about you wait to get on those kennels and we jump into the truck, go over to your friend's house, and get one now."

Wren's shoulders dropped and she smiled. She could always count on Landry.

He started for the door, turned back, and covered the container of brownies, slipping them into his bottom drawer. "You know, in case anybody drops by."

oひo

Susan eyes lit up when she opened the door. She was so grateful they'd come to her and wanted to find out who hurt J.R. that she hugged them both. Poor little J.R. was lying in the middle of a puffy comforter on the sofa. Susan pulled back his new blanket to show them the extent of his injuries—hind end shaved bare, a zigzag of angry black stitches down his leg, plastic cone on his head. Wren winced. Thankfully, his meds had him conked, so they didn't bother him. They all took a seat.

"I got most of the details of what happened from Wren, ma'am," Landry said as he handed her the clipboard, incident report form, and a pen. "If you would just fill out the personal information on the top and sign the bottom...No promises, but we'll definitely see what we can do."

Susan took the clipboard. As she was writing, she shook her head. "Seems like it will be almost impossible to find them, but I sure appreciate you trying." She finished the form, handed it to Landry, then reached to stroke J.R.'s back ever so gently. "I'm just so lucky to still have him. Wren...honey...I can't thank you enough."

Landry smiled and put a hand on Wren's shoulder. "Yep.

Guess I better keep this one around." He turned to Wren. "And we better be getting back to the shelter." He nodded at Susan. "We'll be in touch if we find anything."

Susan stood, hugged them both again, and walked them to the door.

They climbed back into the truck. Landry slammed his door. As he pulled out of the driveway, he shook his head. "What a piece of crap."

His jaw clenched. His knuckles went white on the steering wheel. "You gotta be pretty worthless as a human being to do something like that. Why not do the world a favor and shoot yourself instead?!"

He stopped at the end of the street and cut his eyes over to Wren as if he'd forgotten she was with him. He scrunched up his face and shrugged. "Oops, sorry. I shouldn't have said that... It's just—"

Wren, who had been watching him, raised a hand to signal *no apology necessary*. "It's okay. I get it." She appreciated that what happened to J.R. had upset him—definitely a much better reaction than her dad's. But she got the feeling this wasn't all about J.R. Something else was eating at him. She chewed her bottom lip. She'd ask what—ask if maybe she could help, but it would kill her if he said something like, *Thanks, but you're just a kid. What can you do?* She didn't really think he would... but he might. And sure, he'd frame it nicer, because that was Landry, but it wouldn't make it hurt any less. In fact, coming from Landry, it would probably hurt even more. She propped her elbow on the door, put her hand under her chin, and turned toward the window. She sighed, deciding the best and safest course of action was to stay silent.

They pulled up to the shelter. Landry put the truck in park and turned off the key. He looked at the steering wheel for a moment, then over at Wren. "Hey, I'm really sorry. That was a terrible thing for me to say. I didn't mean it." He paused. "There's been several incidents of abuse lately and I...just..." He shook his head. "It's just been tough."

Wren's jaw dropped. "Several? What—"

Landry didn't answer. Just grabbed his stuff, got out of the truck, and headed for the office.

Wren followed him, wanting to know more. The shelter phone was ringing as they walked in the door. Landry snatched it from across the desk. "Animal shelter," he said. His brow furrowed. He tucked the phone under his chin, pulled his cell phone from his back pocket, and scrolled through his missed messages. "Yeah, I got them," he said gravely. "Turned my ringer off to take a report. Be right there."

He hung up the phone. "I need to go."

She had a million questions racing through her mind, but all she said was, "I'll do the kennels."

"Thanks," he said and was out the door.

She rolled up her sleeves and gathered the needed supplies—gloves, hose, broom, disinfectant, squeegee, and trash bags—from the closet and went to work. The million questions were still there, for sure, but just like all the other times her mind kicked into overdrive—about her mom, about school, about everything—poop-scooping helped calm the crazy. She always joked with Landry about kennel cleaning being a "crap" job, but it was one she didn't mind. Sure, it was unglamorous, and stinky without a doubt, but to her, going through all the steps to make sure each of their spaces were clean and sanitary was a very personal way to care for these sweet, forgotten souls. A way to show them some love. Plus—bonus—she got paid in purrs, wagging tails, and kisses. How was that not worth it?

She had finished up, had her jacket on, and was getting ready to leave when she heard Landry's truck pull in. She went to the door and watched as he slid a small black plastic bag onto the tailgate.

Her eyes went to the flat plastic bag. She knew what that meant. He'd found an animal beyond help and now had to properly dispose of the poor thing. Her hand went to her mouth. The thought of him having to deal with that made her heart hurt. She took a step back from the door for some distance. Oh yeah, she'd much rather clean kennels. But even worse, that bag…it also made her think of J.R. How it could've been his little body inside that bag if she'd been even a minute later.

She could hide, act like she hadn't seen, but that wouldn't be right. She stepped outside. "Hey," she said softly.

"Hey, kiddo." His voice was flat.

Wren knew Landry hated this part of his job. Who wouldn't? But all you had to do was spend ten seconds with him to know how much pride he took in his work—how much he truly cared for all animals. Unfortunately, most of the time, more than their so-called owners did.

She shook her head. Just watching it was painful.

But as much as she knew any dead animal bothered Landry, this one must be worse than usual. She could see it in his steeled eyes and his set-again jaw. He was angry.

Wren moved to the tailgate. "Bad?"

Landry dropped his head. "Worst I've ever seen." He hesitated as if trying to decide how much he should tell her, but only for a moment. That was another thing she liked about Landry. He may call her kiddo, but he didn't treat her like one.

"Tabby. At least I think so. Someone hurt it so badly, it's hard to tell. Got an anonymous tip. Found it taped to a fence." Landry's eyes went dim like he was seeing the horrific scene all over again. "Trust me, that's as much as you want to know."

Wren's jaw dropped along with her stomach. The air around them was gone.

Landry looked over at what must have been her pale face. "Oh my gosh…Sorry…" He shook his head. "I guess I just needed…" His eyes widened and he held up his hands. "Holy—don't, do not tell the chief I told you anything. I'd be out on my as—uh—bee-hind for sure."

Saying nothing, unable to make her brain work, she kept shaking her head. When she was finally able to form words, there was only one that came out. "Why?"

Landry sighed. "Darlin', I gave up trying to figure that one out a long time ago." He ran his hand down his face. "I don't know what's going on…"

They stood there for the longest time, staring at the poor cat in the bag. She placed her hand gently on the bag and said a quick prayer. Landry nodded, then carefully picked the bag up and carried it inside the shelter.

Wren wanted to help Landry, but her feet wouldn't follow. She just wasn't that strong. Distance—as much as possible—from the dead body was what was needed to loosen the fist-sized knot in her stomach. She felt her eyes fill, and the tears fall. She dragged her jacket sleeve across her face, and without saying bye, grabbed her bike and headed home.

◌ ⊘ ◌

When she got to the house, she found her dad engrossed in his office and Elisi's truck gone. She snuck into her room without notice. She jammed a pillow over her face, trying to suffocate the gruesome pictures she'd conjured up in her head. That poor, poor cat. What it must have gone through. She curled up on her side, hugging the pillow and wondered... *How sick would a person have to be?*

How sick was the person who took her mother?

Grisly what-if pictures assaulted her. Imaginary, her brain knew. Still, she wanted to scream. A loud, long, primal scream that would scare away everything in a three-block radius. But she couldn't. Not here. Not now. Not ever. Everybody would hear and come running. And the discussions of therapy, support groups, or someone-you-can-talk-tos, would resume and really drive her over the edge.

She threw the pillow to the floor. She needed to calm down, needed to find a way to reel herself in. Spiraling was out of the question. She lay on her back and took three deep breaths.... In through her nose...out through her mouth...Like Elisi had shown her.

"What we conjure in our heads is always worse than reality, Usdi. Don't go down that dark path. We must have faith the spirits will reveal the truth to us when the time is right. When we are ready to hear it." Elisi had closed her eyes, turned up her palms, and led by example. "Until then, we breathe in...and breathe out..."

But this time, the whole deep breathing thing wasn't helping. Wren pulled the covers up over her head. *Faith*. She scoffed at the thought. Faith could only be there if there was an upside. But was there? Really? She wasn't stupid. Either her mom had met some horrible fate or she'd just out-and-out left them. Left her. Her hands wadded the edges of her blanket. No, her mom would never, ever do that. Wren knew that as sure as she knew her own name.

She felt it.

If her mom was able, she would come home.

She kneaded the knot in her stomach with the heel of her hand. Maybe she was the reason the spirits held their secrets. Maybe if she was a better person. A better daughter. A better Cherokee...

She blew out her breath and threw the covers off from her head. Or maybe—probably—she was just crazy. After all, wasn't it crazy to want an answer when you know that very answer will most likely break you?

She shook her head. Still, she had to know. She couldn't help it. She just couldn't—wouldn't quit.

Not like her dad. He hadn't come right out and said so, but Wren was pretty sure he'd already given up. All the coming straight home from the station—shutting himself up in the office he'd made from the extra bedroom. Elisi constantly reminding him he needed to eat, having to leave a tray outside the door because he'd made it clear no one else was allowed inside. No. All the long nights of the light shining under his office door, turning over rocks, searching for clues, had stopped some time ago. Wren had overheard him on the phone. *"I have to focus on what's best for us now."*

She didn't get to hear the rest of his side of the conversation. Maybe *his* gut feeling sensed her right outside, or she'd unknowingly made a sound, but he yanked open his office door and saw her standing in the hallway.

He hadn't gotten angry. If anything, his face said he understood. It was no secret Wren was always looking for answers. He just cut the caller off, kissed the top of her head, and told her she should be in bed. "You've got school tomorrow."

And that was that.

So, she'd gone to her room and gotten back into bed. But all she could hear or think about, were her dad's words, ... *what's best for us now...*

What she wanted to say—what she wanted to yell at him—was: *Isn't finding Mom what's best for us? Isn't it the only thing?*

Wren never had the nerve to ask him point-blank if he'd backed off the search. Not that he would tell her anyway. Sometimes she'd catch herself staring at him. Watching him work at his desk or in front of the TV. Trying her best to use that gut instinct thing to read whatever was going on in his mind. Trying to figure out how she could love him so much, but sometimes hate him. No, she shoved that question down and filed it under not ready to hear the answer. The benefit, without knowing for sure, was she could keep pretending things were the same. That finding her mom was still his number one priority. Like it was hers. Like it was Elisi's.

It hurt too much to think it wasn't.

It was of some comfort at least that dropping the investigation would never be her dad's decision. Cases couldn't be officially closed until there was a definitive answer. So, even if he wanted to focus on other things, her mom's case would remain open. And open equals hope....Even when it grows cold. And even though Wren's head told her something bad had probably happened, her heart...her heart just couldn't give up.

Chapter Ten

The next few days were spent on autopilot. Once again, Wren went to her desk and turned on her laptop. She clicked on Google Alerts and started down her memorized list:

- Carjacking
- Missing woman found
- Native remains

She scanned the results, clicking on any in and around Oklahoma. She knew, technically, her mom could be anywhere, but she had to narrow it down—she had to start somewhere.

She sat back in her chair and chewed on her pencil. As usual, none of the records were worth digging into deeper, plus she was tired. She steered the cursor to Internet settings and deleted her browsing history. A pain, but her dad checked regularly to make sure she was being "safe." She finished the session off with a few bogus clicks to her email, the school web page, and a couple of other harmless sites, so it wouldn't be obvious what she'd been up to.

She sat back and stared at the screen, watching the blink of the cursor on the blank page. It waited patiently, as if knowing she had something she wanted to say. And as she'd done so many times, she reached for the keys and typed a message she had no place to send.

I MISS YOU.

She sighed, clicked off the computer, and crashed back onto her bed, the headboard hitting hard against the wall. She buried her face in her hands, then dragged them back through her hair. She was so very sick of having nothing but questions.

The fact that her finder feelings were useless when it came to her mom was nothing but a cruel joke. It had to be, right? Or maybe it was a punishment? But what could she have possibly done in twelve short years that would make God do such a thing?

She scoffed. At least that gut instinct thing of hers worked well enough to tell her that couldn't be it. That was something, she guessed. But...He is God...Couldn't He at least point her in the right direction?

It's not like she hadn't asked Him. But her prayers, like her questions, went unanswered.

Elisi had a theory. "You are a finder of lost things, Usdi. This is true. But your mother's energy is all around us—in us." Her eyes shimmered with sadness, reminding Wren she wasn't the only one in pain. Elisi patted her heart. "How can she be lost when she's right here?"

Wren guessed that made sense. At least it helped her feel less like a complete finding failure, so she decided to cling to it.

Elisi was right, it would be hard for anyone not to sense her mom around. There were reminders everywhere.

The crooked river cane basket atop the mantel her mom had learned to make in a class.

The throw, across the arm of the sofa, she used to keep her feet warm.

Assorted frames around the house holding frozen moments of happier times...before. The favorite memories her mom had immortalized behind plates of glass....A chubby baby Wren learning how to swim, her mom kissing away the droplets of water that clung to her lashes. Wren, her mom, and her dad posing like touristy nerds in front of a massive redwood tree in Northern California.

But Wren's all-time favorite picture was the one on her bedside table. Just the two of them, her and her mom. An impromptu selfie taken at Diligwa, the replica of a real Cherokee village outside Tahlequah. Both in plain old gray sweatshirts, time-of-their-life smiles, and brand-new, identical, custom-made turquoise stones on sterling chains. Made especially for them by a famous Cherokee artisan friend of her mom's. The same one who had begged her mom to give up trying to learn basketweaving.

"Maybe you should stick with buying Native art," he had teased her.

It was this picture that helped keep her grounded. Anytime Wren entertained the crazy notion her mom might have chosen to leave her—something that had been thrown in her face at school—she needed only to pick up this picture, run her fingertips across the glass, and take herself back to this day.

Elisi popped her head into her bedroom. "Still up?" She walked over and slipped the photo from Wren's hand. She smiled as she stared at it for a little while. She kissed her fingers and pressed them on the picture. "My sweet, sweet girls." She placed the frame back on the table, leaned over, and kissed Wren on the forehead. "It is so late, Usdi. *This* is why you aren't a morning person."

Wren shrugged. "Can't help it. Besides, there are studies that say night owls are more creative and have higher IQs." She acted like she was going to get up. "Here, I can show you—"

Elisi stopped her with her hand. She shook her head. "Right. There are studies that say anything you want them to say," she said as she walked to the door and started to pull it closed. "Now, go to sleep. I have no interest in making breakfast for a half-white zombie."

Wren held up a hand in concession. She reached over and turned off the lamp, bathing the room in the moon's bluish glow. Most nights she found it soothing, but not tonight. Tonight, it just felt eerie. She stared at the ceiling, not wanting to close her eyes. Each time she tried, images of that poor tortured cat in a black plastic bag and J.R.'s little body on a bloody flannel shirt kept assaulting the backs of her eyelids. Somebody had killed that cat on purpose, and somebody meant to kill J.R. And Landry had said there were others?

She sat bolt upright. "What if the same person is responsible for all of them?"

The minute she said it out loud, in every cell of her body, it felt true. The pit of her stomach, the depths of her soul—wherever it was her finder feelings resided, she knew she was right.

The plaque of the Wolf Clan at the museum flashed in her mind, her own words rang in her ears. *We. Are. Protectors.*

She had to do something. She had to protect these poor animals, just as her ancestors would have. Such a cruel, heartless, purely evil person had to be stopped.

But first, she had to find them.

Chapter Eleven

Wren's eyes once again were glued to the clock at the front of the classroom. The second hand was no match for her fidgety leg. She needed to get to the shelter to talk to Landry.

The bell rang.

She grabbed her backpack and her jacket off the back of her chair, and was almost clear of the North Ed Building when she came face-to-face with Meagan Jacobs—aka M.J.—which, if you were to ask Wren, and just about everybody stuck in the no-man's land of middle school, stood for Mammoth Jerk.

M.J. was a junior at Fort Gibson High, representative of the student council, only daughter of Fort Gibson's Mayor Jacobs, and the absolute worst kind of bully. A master at disguising an insult behind the flash of perfect pearly whites, she was a walking cheap shot wrapped in a smile. Wren would much rather just get punched.

M.J.'s long auburn curls bounced as she walked down the hall, her head moving back and forth as if giving everyone ample opportunity to see her. In reality, she was scanning the target-rich environment for her next victim. Seeing as how Wren was one her favorites, Wren braced herself.

This was the bad thing about the North Ed Building. Middle school and high school both had classes. In. The. Same. Building.

Two completely different species, genetically designed NOT to interact with each other, forced, by no fault of their own, to roam the same halls.

It's a wonder any middle schooler got out alive.

M.J., with her trademark fake smile plastered across her face, bounced her hair over to Wren. "Ooh, Wren, that's such a cute shirt. I absolutely adore it." She raised a finger to her chin as if to look thoughtful. "I had one just like it, but I think my mom gave it to Goodwill."

What could Wren say to that? Thank you? Instead, she mimicked M.J. and put her finger on her chin and, just for a second, imagined giving M.J. a long-deserved throat punch, then shook her head. "Nah, couldn't be yours." She hooked her thumb under the shoulder seam of the shirt and matched M.J.'s fake smile. "It's way too small."

"Yeah." M.J. snorted. "In the boobs."

The two girls who followed M.J. everywhere—minion one and minion two—howled as the three walked off in triumph.

Wren rolled her eyes and hitched her backpack up on her shoulder. She had meant too small to fit over her big-inflated-ego head, but whatever. Just once she'd like to unleash the full fury of her finely tuned sarcastic wit and reduce M.J. to a whimpering, melting heap of hatefulness, much like the Wicked Witch of the West. But she couldn't. She might be able to get away with smarting off a little here and there—just enough to maintain some degree of dignity—but being the only precious daughter of the mayor meant that M.J.'s dad was Wren's dad's boss. And that was a whole new level of trouble she didn't need.

She wheeled into the shelter. Landry's truck wasn't there. He kept the office open during business hours when out on the road so that if somebody was going to dump an animal, at least the poor thing would be safe inside.

She bit on her bottom lip, trying to decide if she should go in and snoop around. She wanted to. *Really* wanted to. Her finder feelings, sixth sense, or whatever, was on high alert, and patience wasn't exactly one of her virtues. Since last night, she'd grown even more convinced that J.R., the cat, and the other abuse cases were all connected.

Her first instinct had been to run it past Landry—get his opinion—see what he thought they should do next. But what if he didn't want her help? She sat back on her bike seat. Or worse, he didn't believe her? A conspiracy theory from a kid who watches too much true crime TV. Or BEYOND worse, he mentioned it to her dad?

Nope. She shook her head. First, she needed proof.

She propped her bike against the fence. If she could get a look at the other abuse reports, look into them a little herself, put together what was going on, then she could bring it to Landry.

That was the plan. But she stopped at the doorway of his office and chewed on her thumbnail. She didn't mind snooping in her dad's office—that was his own fault. He brought it on himself for not answering her questions. But the thought of digging around Landry's office, his personal space, made her all queasy. Landry trusted her. To care for the animals, to be at the shelter when he wasn't there. But then, she'd never given him any excuse not to. Until now.

The barks, and whines, and whimpers begged for attention

the second she'd stepped inside. She couldn't resist. She turned and headed for the kennels. If she was going to invade Landry's privacy, at least she should try to atone for it first.

She checked on water, scratched behind ears, and said little prayers that each would soon find a home. But no matter how long she stayed, they always craved more. One more rub of a belly. One more *Good boy* or *Good girl*. Cage after cage after cage, the story was the same.

She latched the last gate and walked back to the office, taking a quick look out front to make sure the coast was still clear. She slipped behind the desk and riffled through the messy stacks of papers and files on the desk, uncovering an empty brownie container. The bad news...Landry's system, if you could call it one, was the complete opposite of her dad's everything-in-its-place. The good news...she wouldn't have to worry about putting things back exactly where she'd found them.

There were stacks of everything...adoption contracts, foster applications, spay and neuter flyers. She stopped short when she came across a voluntary surrender form for the ten-year-old chocolate Lab she'd seen in the back. He was scared, confused, wondering what he'd done wrong. She couldn't even get him to raise his head. Now she knew why. He'd been dumped by the only family he'd ever known because they no longer wanted the responsibility. Sure, they were moving, had a new baby, or some other lame excuse, but that's what it boiled down to. The voluntary surrender form should really be called unable to honor commitment form. She crinkled the form in her hand.

Some people just suck.

The desk was a bust. She looked around, and spotted a tray labeled INCIDENT REPORTS—TO BE FILED on top of the cabinet.

AHA! Okay, so a little bit of a system. She leafed through the stack and found J.R.'s report and three other incidents of abuse in as many months plus two more inside the top drawer. That was six incidents since the first of the year. Something was definitely going on. Something terrible.

She fished her phone out of her back pocket, snapped pictures of the six reports, and put them all back. The file drawer clicked shut just as she heard the sound of tires crunching the gravel out front.

Landry's face lit up when he saw her. "Hey, kiddo."

If she looked like she'd just been caught doing something, he didn't seem to notice. He held up the carrier he had in his hand. Three tiny, pointy-eared heads and six big green eyes stared out at her.

"Awww..." Wren waggled her fingers in the universal sign for *Gimme*. She took the carrier from him and stuck her face in the front of the grate. "Three babies? How old?"

Landry dropped his duffel bag onto the side chair and sat his drink on his desk, shoving a stack of papers aside to first make room. "Nope, four. Mr. Shy-likable is in the back there. Not sure. Maybe two or three weeks. Poor little tykes have lost their mama."

"Yeah..." Wren deadpanned, "there's a lot of that going around."

That would've made most people stumble all over themselves, but not Landry. He did a little half chuckle and gave her a *Good-one* nod.

She shrugged, proud of herself. After all, Elisi had told her, "If you can't laugh, all you'll do is cry." She was just applying the life lesson.

"Cherokees have a great sense of humor," Elisi told her

61

more than once. "It's one of the things that has helped our people endure. Take me, for instance. I'm hysterical." She raised her chin and turned her head from side to side. "And agiwoduhi, to boot!" She leaned toward Wren, with a cocked eyebrow. "That means 'I am beautiful,'" she said in her you-would-know-that-if-you-studied-our-language way.

Landry's voice brought her back to the moment. "Didn't expect you here. What's up?"

"Oh, I, uh, I was at the library and thought I'd check the cages for you." She went back to playing with the kittens so he couldn't read the lie on her face. Lie? Okay, technically, she did check the cages and, if she stopped by the library on the way home, even if she only rode through the parking lot, then it wouldn't really be a lie—just the truth told out of order.

Being forced to investigate her mom's case on her own had made her pretty good at strategically manipulating the truth. And although it probably wasn't something to include on her college applications, or something she should be all that proud of, there was no arguing, it could be a very useful skillset. Besides, in her experience, most adults didn't really want to hear the whole truth anyway. It made them nervous.

But right now, she was the one feeling nervous. That tickle in the pit of her stomach that tried, so frequently, to tell her to hold on, wait a second, think before making your next move had kicked in. That flitter of internal wisdom she hadn't quite mastered the art of listening to. She chewed the inside of her cheek, to the point of tasting a hint of blood, and tried to decide what she should do next. She came here wanting to share her suspicions with Landry. To get his help. To catch a serial abuser together. To at least be able to solve one mystery in her life.

But suspicions based on nothing more than feelings was exactly that...nothing. And she couldn't face the thought of him thinking she was a Froot Loop. It was a sad, sad state of seventh-grade affairs, but Landry was basically Wren's only friend, and she didn't want to risk losing him.

So that was that. The wrestling match in her head had been officially decided. For now, her theories would tap out.

Just like the other mystery she had in her life. She'd figure this one out on her own.

Chapter Twelve

She had a plan. She burst through the front door and headed straight for her room.

"Thirty-minute warning!" Elisi hollered after her.

Wren screeched to a halt and backed up. "What?"

Elisi pulled the lid off the large stainless pot on the stove. A waft of cloudy steam swirled to the ceiling. The pungent, earthy smell of simmering beans hit Wren, full force, right in the nostrils. Beans. The only food she'd ever known that looked, smelled, and unfortunately tasted just like their name. Brown. To say Wren wasn't a fan was an understatement.

But her dad was, so this must mean he was actually coming home for dinner. Thank the good Lord above the beans were always accompanied with Elisi's Famous Sweet Yellow Corn Bread.

Wren leaned over the pot and wrinkled her nose. Elisi waved her off with the dish towel she had in her hand. "Your dad will be gone for the rest of the week and I want to send him off with one of his favorites. It won't kill you."

Wren mock gagged and backed away from the stove. "It might."

Then a realization hit her—why her dad was coming home for dinner. A little quality family time before once again heading out the door. Flying out for some police chief conference somewhere. A conference where a complete stranger could walk up and ask for any updates on her mom's case and her dad would spill his guts—or the beans, pun intended—all because they had the same job description.

Okay...so...maybe a complete stranger wouldn't know to ask about his wife's disappearance, but still, she knew what she meant. It was crap. All of it. It was brown too.

Elisi sprinkled in a bit more seasoning, gave the beans a healthy stir, and replaced the lid. "Go wash up now. Your dad will be here soon, and you smell like dog."

Wren threw open her arms and headed toward Elisi to give her a big hug.

Elisi lifted her spoon to block her. "Back, dog child, back." But then she chuckled and cocked her head so Wren could kiss her cheek.

"Better a dog than those mangy brown beans," Wren teased as she headed toward her room, the sound of Elisi's laughter behind her.

❧❦❧

Dinner was uncomfortable, to say the least. Wren knew her dad was trying, covering all the basics. *How was your day? Do anything special? Any plans while I'm gone?*

Wren's one-word answers hung in the air. *Fine. No. Nope.* She knew she was being a butthead, but she couldn't help it. Sometimes it was just too much. She didn't know why this was one of those times. It just was. She dropped her spoon; it clanked on her plate. "Are you ever going to tell us anything about Mom?" Her voice strained into a cry. "Are you even looking for her? Do you even care?"

"Wren!" Elisi's voice was stern. "Do not speak to your father that way."

Wren's eyes blurred with her tears. Still, she could see the hurt she had inflicted.

Her dad nodded at Elisi and cleared his throat. "It's all right. I understand the frustration that she—that both of you must feel."

Elisi folded her napkin neatly and placed it beside her plate. Her smile tightened. "I appreciate the sentiment, William. But you do not understand. You can't. We are the only ones left to suffer in the dark. If there is any new information, you know instantly. And, depending on what it is, we may never be told."

He threw up his hands. "I can't—"

She raised her palm to stop him. "Yes, yes, we know. You can't release information that might compromise an active case. And we understand they may not be telling you everything. That we do know. Very well, thank you. But you also can't blame us if sometimes, your silence feels as if we are being tortured twice."

Wren's jaw dropped. Elisi had never, ever, said anything remotely like that to her dad—at least not in front of her. It was exactly what she wanted to say, only she hadn't known how to say it. Or maybe just never had the guts to.

Her dad's phone rang—literally, saving him by the bell. But that didn't matter. Elisi had given Wren's pain and frustration a voice. Now he knew how she felt. How they both felt. That alone made her feel better. Wren's heart swelled. Her admiration for Elisi had skyrocketed through the roof straight into the stratosphere. She slathered a piece of Elisi's Famous Sweet Yellow Corn Bread with butter, took a bite, and smiled. Her grandmother was one Cherokee badass.

Chapter Thirteen

Wren pulled her English book from her locker, shut the door with a clank, and spun the combination, all in one smooth move.

The bell rang as she tugged on the classroom door. She sucked in her breath and slinked to her seat. Mrs. Myers, luckily, busy with the paper cutter, didn't notice. What's that saying? *Sorry I'm late, but I didn't want to be here.* Boy, was that ever the truth.

Ordinarily, Mrs. Myers's English class was one of Wren's favorites. Assignments were normally done on their laptops, so, for the most part, her desk in the back row gave her an hour of uninterrupted Internet—in search of the next "Missing" site that might have information. She wasn't sure how closely the school monitored their browsing—not exactly something she could ask—so she used the hot spot on her phone just to be safe. Luckily, her dad had never questioned the usage. A bridge she'd cross when she came to it.

She was quite good at minimizing and switching screens to whatever she was supposed to be doing whenever Mrs. Myers went on patrol and ended up behind her. Wren was pretty sure Mrs. Myers had caught her a time or two, but nothing came of it. Guess the whole vanishing parent thing made teachers uncomfortable too.

But on this fine fall day, as she looked out the window, at the gloomy, overcast sky, English class would most definitely NOT be Wren's favorite. Mrs. Myers was about to commence with the drawing for project partners.

Partner…She sighed. The very word made her stomach cramp. She was better alone. It's what she was used to. Besides, she had more important things to do than some useless assignment on conjugating verbs or whatever. She had a plan—a mission—at least the beginnings of one to catch whoever had hurt J.R. and the others.

"E-liz-a-beth." Mrs. Myers would say each student's name as she wrote it, then fold the thin strip of paper and drop it into the big glass bowl on her desk.

"Josh-u-a."

"Ran-dee-with-an-E."

"Ran-dy-with-a-Y."

Wren winced. It was downright painful.

Finally, when Mrs. Myers was done, she smiled, held up the bowl, and swirled the contents like she was giving away a grand prize instead of randomly tying Wren to some other body for the next four weeks.

Mrs. Myers sat the bowl back down on her desk. Her eyes twinkled. "Let the games begin," she said as she drew out the first slip.

Moans, groans, and eye rolls coursed through the room.

Jason Walters, self-proclaimed class entertainer, raised his hand.

Mrs. Myers shot him a what-is-it-now look. "Yes, Jason?"

"Um…games, Mrs. Myers? I don't think that word means what you think it means. Maybe we should look it up."

The room broke out in snorts and snickers. For a second, Wren swore even the corners of Mrs. Myers's mouth cracked a hint of a grin.

"All right, all right," Mrs. Myers said. "Keep it down." She went to the bookcase, pulled the red, worn, three-inch thick, actual Webster's dictionary from the shelf, walked over, and dropped it onto Jason's desk. "Excellent idea, Mr. Walters. You should do that. And while you're at it, look up *vainglorious*, and write the class a riveting story that embodies its meaning. I trust you'll have no problem with a main character. Two hundred and fifty words by Friday. Need I spell it?"

Oohs and *uh-ohs* joined the spatter of stifled laughter.

Poor Jason, Wren thought. He just never seemed to learn. Mrs. Myers doesn't play.

She went back to the bowl again and re-mixed the names with her hand, and shot Jason a look as if to say, *Try me.*

Wren's foot wouldn't stay still. Her stomach churned. Further confirmation she should've brought her lunch from home and steered clear of the smothered steak in the cafeteria. She wiped her sweaty palms on her jeans. What would happen when her name was read? More groans? More eye rolls? Whispered pleas of her forced-partner begging to trade? She wrapped her arms around her backpack and hugged it to her chest. A school-made shield of nylon, books, and paper.

Still, it could be worse. Mrs. Myers could've told everyone to buddy up or find a friend, in which case Wren would've unzipped the flap on her backpack, shoved it over her head, and tried to suffocate herself.

"Wren, you are partnered with..."

Hearing her name jolted her back to the moment. Her mouth

went dry. Unsure what to do, she pulled out her notebook and picked up her pen, as if she was incapable of committing the next name read out loud to memory.

"Brantley."

Head still down, she cut her eyes over to Brantley Sims, two rows over, three rows up. Oh God, he was looking right at her.

But there was no moan. No groan. No eye roll. Just a nod of acknowledgment in her direction. Her shoulders lowered, her whole body relaxed, and she started to breathe again.

She didn't really know Brantley all that well. They had gone to school together since the second grade, when his family moved to Fort Gibson from somewhere—she couldn't remember. But that year was when Wren's world turned upside down. In a way, that year, Wren also disappeared. It's hard to make friends, let alone keep them, when all you really want to be is invisible.

Chapter Fourteen

It was back to her plan, the plan before a confrontational brown bean dinner and a pointless English assignment with some kid who was basically a stranger, had tried to derail her.

"A shared legacy: how to work together to leave a mark." Mrs. Myers had stood before the class, her face full of that inspired look teachers get when they think they have a great idea for expanding young minds. Judging by her smile, she thought she'd just won a Pulitzer.

Mrs. Myers stopped in front of each row and counted out the proper number of guideline sheets as she explained the project that would monopolize the next month of their lives. Four weeks to prepare a *No-less-than-ten and no-more-than-twenty-minute oral presentation with their partner.* She peered over the top of her reading glasses, watching, making sure everybody had a copy, then headed back to her desk. She rubbed her hands together. "I can't wait to see what each team comes up with. You know what they say about two minds...."

Wren tore the sheet of the random keep-her-head-down scribbles from her notebook, wadded it up, and tossed it in the trash can on her way out. She, on the other hand, most definitely could wait. She had more important things to tend to.

Animal-lifesaving things. And this English assignment was a Major League inconvenience. Wren breezed past Brantley without giving him or this stupid project a second thought.

But on the bike ride home, an idea suddenly hit her. She could use this assignment as an excuse. The first part of her catch-an-animal-abuser plan was to make a crime board just like she'd seen so many times on TV. Not on the computer that her dad might find, but an old-school, real-life, in the flesh murder board like a real private eye or detective would do.

It would be easy since her dad was out of town. There was a big whiteboard at the shelter in the storage room that she was sure Landry would let her borrow. Once it was in her room, she'd be scot-free. Her dad always knocked on her door and gave her plenty of time to answer—the idea of walking in on any girl stuff made him nervous. And plenty of time to answer, meant plenty of time to cover her tracks.

As she wheeled up to her house, the pieces had pretty much fallen together.

"I'm home!" she announced as if the slamming door behind her wasn't a dead giveaway.

Elisi was sitting on the sofa in the family room, engrossed in a breaking news bulletin on the TV. Wren walked up behind her, resting her hands on her grandmother's shoulders. Elisi patted Wren's hand, but said nothing, intent on the images on the screen.

Wren made her way around to the front of the sofa and sat down beside her.

"*Missing teen…Search parties…Flyers…Community devastated…Outpouring of support…*" The reporter spoke over picture after picture of a pretty, fair-skinned missing girl and her pretty white smile. The same pictures they'd seen in so many places for the last several weeks. She stiffened.

Elisi clicked off the TV.

Wren shook her head.

Elisi reached for her hand.

This was nothing new. It happened every time the news blasted repeated requests for help locating a missing loved one. A nationally televised reminder that most of these call to arms were reserved for those who looked a certain way.

Not like her mother.

At first, whenever she saw these stories, Wren couldn't help herself. She would set her jaw, ball her fists, and direct the searing ball of anger inside her at the missing person. Like it was somehow their fault they were getting all the attention her mother had deserved when she'd first gone missing. Like maybe if all those people would've pitched in to help—would've cared—they might have been able to find her.

"Oh, baby girl." Elisi had slipped an arm around Wren and told her a long time ago. "The people who are missing are not to blame. It is the fault of those who think it's their job to tell us what and who matters. We are only to blame if we listen."

Wren sat there in silence and tried to remember that.

Elisi slapped her hands on her knees, "Well, that's enough of that. Let's get you a snack, shall we? A little something sweet before dinner?"

"Nah, I'm good, thanks." She held up her hands and crossed her fingers. "But I sure could use a ride to the shelter. I've got a really big project in English, and I need to borrow the whiteboard Landry keeps in the storage room. And it's too big to carry on my bike." She never said the whiteboard was actually for the English project, so technically, everything she'd said was true.

"Landry say you could?"

"I'm sure it's okay, he's not using it, but I'll text him to double-check."

Elisi stood up. "Just let me get my purse and find my…" She patted her pockets and scanned the coffee and side tables. "Keys…"

Wren closed her eyes and pressed her fingers against her temples as if psychically trying to connect with the keys. Elisi's losing them was somewhat of a frequent occurrence, so Wren having to "tap in" to them happened frequently as well. The trick was doing it without laughing. She jumped up, pecked Elisi on the cheek, and headed toward the kitchen. She scanned the room and—TA-DA!—found the keys by the fridge next to the grocery sack on the counter.

Elisi shook her head in amazement. "I'll never understand how you do that. But I sure am glad you can."

Wren stifled a grin. What Elisi didn't know or had long since forgotten, is that since she was forever misplacing her keys, her dad had bought one of those little square tracker things for her key ring. At first, Wren had put the app on her own phone to help, knowing Elisi would never figure out how to work it, but at some point, just kidding around, she'd used it to pretend her finder feelings were supernatural. Elisi had fallen for it, Wren had sworn her dad to secrecy, and she'd been having fun with it ever since. Wren hadn't really closed her eyes to tune in to the missing key spirits. She was glancing down at the app on her phone.

Elisi grabbed the keys out of Wren's hand. "Let's go!"

Wren knew Landry was probably out on patrol, so she called him on the way instead.

"Help yourself, but I expect a mention in the project acknowledgments—or more of your grandmother's brownies." He paused. "Yeah...strike the acknowledgment. I'd rather have the brownies."

Wren chuckled. "You got it."

They pulled up to the shelter. Landry was still out in his truck, but like usual, she knew the door would be open.

Elisi turned the truck off. "I'll wait out here and keep the truck warm. I can't go in there where all those poor abandoned babies are. I'd bring every single one home." She cocked a brow. "Your father would not approve." She paused. "But...if you need help..."

Wren shook her head. "Nope, I can get it."

Wren felt the same way. But her only option was to love on all the animals—especially the dogs—as much and as often as possible. "Be right back."

As soon as she got inside the door, she hesitated. The storage room gave her the creeps normally, but this time of year, it spooked her more than usual. Somebody at City Hall thought it was the best place to store the full-sized casket they use for the Halloween carnival every year. But it was too late to turn back now. She did a hard swallow, opened the door, and clicked on the overhead light.

If that light so much as flickered, whiteboard or not, she was out of there.

She grabbed the whiteboard fast as she could, slammed the storage room door on her foot in the process, and bolted—with a slight limp—for the door. She wrestled the whiteboard into the bed of the truck, jumped into the passenger seat, and locked the door.

"Everything okay?" Elisi asked. "What's wrong with your foot?"

"Uh—nothing—it's fine—yeah—uh—this'll work perfect," she said with a weak smile. "Thanks."

As Elisi glanced in the rearview mirror and backed up the truck, Wren reached down to discreetly rub her foot. *What I get for messing with the truth.*

ᴏ ᴓ ᴏ

"So," Elisi said as she pulled out onto Ozark Street, "tell me about this board project. Must be a big deal."

Wren's body slumped in a silent groan. Why did she have to ask? She could act as if she didn't hear the question, but that never worked. She might be able bend the truth a little, but she could never, ever, out-and-out lie to Elisi. A well-timed throb of her foot served as a reminder of karmic consequences. If she'd only said English project instead of board project, then maybe... Her mind raced. She wasn't sure what Elisi would think about her non-English-real-reason-for-the-whiteboard project. More importantly, she wasn't sure what she would do.

Wren sighed. And told her the truth. She was never any good at keeping things from Elisi anyway. Eventually, it always came out. Besides, they'd both had enough information withheld for the past five plus years to last a lifetime. No way she could live with herself if she added to it.

Elisi pulled into the driveway and turned off the truck. "Promise me that if you find anything, you'll pass it along to Landry. Nothing on your own. Nothing dangerous."

Wren held her pinkie finger down with her thumb and stuck up the remaining three fingers. "Scout's honor."

Elisi shook her head. "Not funny. That would only count if you'd ever been a Scout. Now, I mean it.... Promise me."

Wren made a big *X* with her finger over her chest. "Okay, fine. Does crossing my heart count? I mean, I do have a heart."

Elisi's brow raised.

Wren leaned over and gave her a peck on the cheek. "Don't worry. I'll be safe. I promise."

Elisi held open the front door for her as she brought in the whiteboard and headed down the hallway, nearly knocking all the pictures off the wall. In her room, she propped the whiteboard on top of her dresser, using Elisi's set of never-used three-pound exercise weights to keep it from sliding.

There. She was official. She had her murder board.

She sent the pictures of the six abuse reports to her printer, then, in date order, taped them up on the board, taking up most of the white space. The board wasn't the big, stand-up kind, like the ones on TV, but she'd make do.

She stepped back and folded her arms. Her head tilted slightly as she pondered the six cases in front of her. Six separate cases. But her gut—her gut told her they should be rolled into one.

Chapter Fifteen

Holed up in her room, on her stomach on her bed, head propped up by her hands, she stared at the murder board. A knock on her door made her jump.

Obviously not as concerned that Wren might be in her underwear as her dad was, Elisi walked on in—with Brantley Sims right behind her. Wren's eyes grew wide as she leaped off the bed and took a quick swipe with her hands through her hair and down her clothes. She looked at Brantley, then back to Elisi. "Geez, Grandma, glad I was dressed."

"It's four o'clock in the afternoon, dear. Why in good heaven's name would you not be?"

Embarrassed, Brantley's eyes cut to the floor then back to Wren. "Sorry to just drop by. I tried to catch you at school today and I don't have your number. Thought we might talk about our project."

"Oh." Elisi's brow shot up as she looked at Wren. "You didn't tell me your friend was helping. Excellent! I feel better about it already." She gestured at the whiteboard. "There you have it. Looks like she's started already." She smiled at them both. "I'm so proud of you two—wanting to help Landry put an end to this terrible animal abuse. It's just heartbreaking."

Wren took Elisi by the shoulders and hurried her toward the hallway, as a very perplexed look washed over Brantley's face. "Not that project, Elisi," Wren said through gritted teeth. "Thanks, I got this."

She turned to see Brantley standing in front of the murder board, reading intently. He looked at her, his brow scrunched as if that might help him understand. He pointed at the board. "What—"

She waved him off. "Oh, that's nothing. Just a hobby."

His eyes went wide. "Your hobby is a tortured cat, a shot dog, and—"

She dropped her head and pinched the bridge of her nose. She sighed, figuring, at this point, telling him the truth was favorable to him telling everybody at school she was a whack job *Thanks, Grandma.*

"Okay," she said. "Not exactly a hobby. It's something I'm looking into." She shrugged. "Like Elisi said...helping Officer Landry find out who's doing this."

His face lit up like he'd gotten what he wanted for Christmas. He stepped closer. "You mean, like a real investigation? You can do that? I mean, I guess, since your dad's the police chief..." He jabbed his thumb toward the board again. "Is this even legal?"

Wren put out her hands to stop him. "Slow down, lawyer boy. I'm not doing anything wrong. Hello...public records... ever hear about it? And my dad has nothing to do with this. He doesn't even know about it. Nobody at school either. And I want to keep it that way. Okay?"

The corner of his mouth turned up and he nodded as if he'd just acquired a new level of respect for his English partner. Or maybe realized he now had a bargaining chip.

He folded his arms. "Okay," he nodded. "I'll keep it quiet. But only if I can help. I want in."

"What? No way."

His shoulders sagged. "Look, I won't say anything either way, I promise. It's just that…" He swallowed hard, a hint of pain in his eyes. "I know what it's like to lose a pet. I just lost…" He shook his head, "Anyway, please? I'd really like to help."

Wren rubbed at her temples. How could she say no to that? If anybody understood loss and needing to do something, it was her. She chewed on her bottom lip. Losing a pet may pale in comparison to a parent in her eyes, but…maybe…loss is loss. She sighed. Besides, he already knew enough to get her into loads of trouble, so she might as well take a chance and trust him. She shook her head. Trusting an almost complete stranger…what was she getting herself into?

"Okay," she finally said. "Fine. But we can't tell AN-Y-BOD-Y. Deal?"

"Deal." His contractual nod of agreement made his bangs fall across his eyes as he smiled.

She smiled back. "For the record," she said as she pointed at the board. "Legal." Then she pointed at him. "Attempted black-mail NOT legal."

They laughed as Elisi walked through the door again, this time bearing a tray of Elisi's Famous Chocolate No-Bake Cookies. "Wasn't sure what you two might want to drink. Is milk too grade school?"

Brantley wasted no time in putting two cookies in one hand and grabbing a third with the other. He raised it toward her. "Milk will be fine, ma'am. Thank you very much."

"All righty then, two cow juices, coming up."

Wren rolled her eyes teasingly. "Welcome to my life."

"Looks pretty good to me." He popped a whole cookie into his mouth, closed his eyes, and chewed slowly. "Mmm... I haven't had these in, like, forever. My mom—" He stopped.

Wren shrugged, figuring he just felt funny talking about his mom because of her mom. "It's okay," she said. "It doesn't bother me."

She could tell by the look on his face that at first, he didn't get what she was talking about. Then the color drained from his face. "Oh, sorry... I didn't..."

He sucked on his teeth to get the last bits of chocolate as if needing the extra time to decide what to tell her. "My mom disappeared, too. Only mine *chose* to. Guess family life wasn't for her—our family, anyway."

He shuffled back and forth, then suddenly stopped. "Sorry. That didn't come out right." His eyes met hers. "Really... Sorry."

Wren could've kicked herself. Here, standing right in front of her, was a prime example of being so wrapped up in her own problems that she's totally unaware of what's going on around her. Brantley's mom running off would've been the equivalent of middle-grade front-page news and she was totally oblivious. Course, even if she knew, what difference would it have made? Being on the receiving end enough herself, she definitely wouldn't have had any interest in all the gossip.

It made her heart hurt—the sadness in his eyes. In her lowest of times, she'd let herself imagine the possibility her mom had walked out and left them. That she was somewhere—anywhere, alive, and happy. But somehow, she knew that wasn't true. And in a way she couldn't explain, that gave her some comfort... knowing, at least, her mom would be here with her if she could.

She looked at Brantley and a lump caught in her throat as she realized how horrible it must be to know any different.

Chapter Sixteen

She took her time, going the long way home from school. The leaves had turned the vibrant colors of fall, but the Oklahoma winds had prematurely set most of them free. They skimmed over the grass, skipped across the streets in front of her, and gathered here and there in mounds that Wren imagined were leafy versions of family reunions.

The crisp air bit her cheeks as she biked through the neighborhoods, checking out the latest additions of jack-o'-lanterns, inflatable monsters, and haunted house decorations. Mr. Baker, who was busy trying to make a skeleton look like it was falling skull-first off the roof, stopped long enough to give her a wave. She waved back.

She loved this time of year. The creepier the better—except clowns. She shuddered. No clowns.

She pedaled past the familiar signs that read TRAIL OF HONOR and on around to the Fort Gibson National Cemetery entrance. Not because of anything to do with Halloween, but because it was one of Wren's favorite places in Fort Gibson. It looked just like the pictures she'd seen of Arlington. The regimented rows of white chiseled headstones on perfectly manicured grounds—as if all those buried brave souls were at attention. Protecting us still.

She hadn't intended to stop, but today she felt drawn to. She tucked her bike behind the gray stone sign at the entrance, slipped her backpack on, and walked to her usual spot—the east end by the bell tower. The real name for it was a *carillon*, she'd read that on the dedication marker, but since she wasn't sure how to pronounce it, she stuck with bell tower.

She dropped her backpack at the base of one of the big oak trees standing sentry. She sat down on the grass, crossed her legs, and marveled at the grounds. Outside the fence, there were leaves everywhere, but inside, not a single one. Inside, it was perfect.

Her eyes landed on a family close by, paying their respects. She watched as the woman kissed her fingers and touched the top of the headstone. The man wrapped his arm around the woman's waist as she silently dabbed her eyes. A little girl stood behind them, holding a tiny American flag.

Intruding on this private family moment made Wren feel uneasy. She retreated farther back against the tree. But she couldn't look away. Couldn't help but put herself in their place. The man and woman—her dad and Elisi. And Wren was the little girl. Standing over her answer. It was terrible, she knew, to even think that way, but sometimes she longed, with everything in her, for a real, physical, place like this that she could come, sit, and talk with her mom, instead of empty whispers into the night sky.

As if hearing Wren's thoughts, the little girl at the gravesite turned and locked eyes with her. Even after the mother grabbed the girl's hand and pulled her toward their car, she wouldn't look away, her mouth forming a perfect little O as her free hand pointed in Wren's direction.

It was weird and made Wren feel funny. But after the family drove off, it hit her. The little girl must've thought she was looking at a ghost. The wispy remains of a real person, hanging around, watching the life of others go by. And the little girl was right. That *was* Wren. But it wasn't who she wanted to be. Not anymore. Not really. Just the brief time with Brantley—him being in her home, talking, joking, as if they were friends, made her want that to be true. Made her want to venture outside of her self-imposed protective shell. She swallowed hard. But that was easier said than done. Just the thought made her queasy. She stood up, brushed the grass off her butt, and grabbed her backpack. *Besides,* she thought as she headed home, *I don't even know how to rejoin the living.*

Chapter Seventeen

The rich, heavy smell of tobacco greeted Wren as she walked in the door. Elisi must have wanted to use the opportunity of her dad being away to do a full-on house blessing. Carpe diem as they say—or the Cherokee equivalent.

Craft stuff was scattered over the kitchen table and Elisi was hard at work. Wren pulled out a chair and joined her. Elisi looked up, her extra-strength reading glasses low on her nose, and smiled big, like she hadn't seen Wren in forever instead of this morning at breakfast. "Usdi! You're just in time." Elisi always smiled at her like that—like seeing Wren was the highlight of her day, which, in turn, made Wren's day. Mutually beneficial warmth and fuzziness.

Wren scanned the supplies on the table. "Whatcha making?"

Elisi's eyes danced as she reached over and squeezed Wren's hand. "Something special for us. Just finished." She picked up a bracelet and slipped it around Wren's wrist, then dropped her head to inspect her work through her readers. "Little too big…," she said, and went about making the adjustment. Wren watched as her grandmother's fingers worked.

A few minutes later, when it was all said and done, they both had on matching bracelets. A single red silk cord with a simple sterling clasp and safety chain.

"Well, what do you think?" Elisi asked.

Wren turned her wrist slowly. "I like it."

"Well, I got to thinking…" Elisi pulled off her readers and sat them on the table. "I know you know all about the Missing Indigenous Women and Girls movement." She tilted her head. "Don't think for a minute I don't know about all your snooping." She gave her a wink. "Don't worry…our secret."

Wren sheepishly shrugged, but since she was busted, she figured she might as well own it. "MMIWG. Missing and Murdered," she said to correct her.

Elisi waved her off, blocking out the murdered part. "Anyway, with the attention our missing girls are finally starting to get, we need to join in. However, I think your dad and your school would have something to say if we wore red handprints across our mouths every day. So…" She held up her wrist. "I made us these. They can be a symbol of solidarity we can wear twenty-four/seven." She paused and ran her hand over the bracelet. "A single cord." Her voice broke. "For the single vibrant thread our family tapestry is missing."

Wren's breath hitched. Tears instantly blurred her eyes. The huge lump in her throat rendered her speechless. Not that it mattered. How something so simple could mean so much was beyond her words anyway. She blew out a long breath and dragged her sleeve across her face. She got up, went over, and threw her arms around her grandma. The one person in the whole wide world who got her. "Correction," Wren said, sniffling her way through the words. "I don't like it—I absolutely love it."

Chapter Eighteen

Wren was clicking through her regular searches checking for updates when the doorbell rang. She snapped her laptop closed. "I got it. It's for me," she yelled, and headed toward the front door. As she reached for the knob, it suddenly struck her how long it had been since she'd uttered those actual words.

She opened the door to find a smiling Brantley, standing outside on the front stoop, backpack slung over his shoulder, hair swept across one eye. If Wren didn't know better, she'd think he was one of the cool kids. But as she'd watched him in class and at school, things like being cool didn't seem to interest him. He talked, ate lunch, was nice to anyone and everyone, clearly ignoring the social lines drawn in middle school. Maybe that wasn't the definition of cool, but it should be.

"Hey," he said with a nod.

Wren returned the nod and swung open the door.

Brantley stepped inside. Elisi walked up to greet him with open arms. "Osiyo, Brantley. Come in, come in."

Brantley gave Wren a quizzical glance.

Wren smiled. "Osiyo—or siyo. It means hello."

"Ah…" He nodded again, this time to Elisi, and smiled. "Osiyo, ma'am."

Elisi put her hand on his shoulder and raised her brow. "Such manners, this one. But no ma'ams here. Please, call me Elisi."

Wren leaned toward him. "That means *grandmother*."

Brantley looked a little unsure.

Wren chuckled. "It's okay. Everybody does."

Elisi motioned him farther in. "Get on in here," she said. "Make yourself at home. You guys hungry?"

Brantley slid his backpack off his shoulder. "Yes ma'am, Elisi. Always."

Elisi laughed. "Close enough. Go on now, I'll bring you something shortly."

Wren punched his arm. "And that means let's go. We've got crimes to solve."

They headed down the hall to Wren's room. The whiteboard, no longer on the dresser, was now strategically propped against the foot of Wren's bed. If they didn't solve the case before her dad got home, or if he came home early, when he knocked, all she'd have to do is pull out the bottom of the board so it would drop flat on the floor and she could slide it right under the bed.

Brantley dropped his backpack on the floor beside the bed. They plopped down on the braided area rug in front of the board. She gestured at the reports she'd taped to the board. "What I've got so far."

Brantley nodded. "Cool. I've got something too." He reached for his backpack. The sleeve on his hoodie hiked up, revealing the edges of an ugly deep purple bruise. He quickly pulled the sleeve down with his other hand, cut his eyes to Wren, then to the floor.

"Whoa." Wren pointed at his wrist although it was obvious

he was self-conscious, but her curiosity wouldn't allow her mouth to stay shut. "What happened?"

Brantley pulled the sleeve down even more. "Aw, no big deal," he shrugged. "War wound. Bike fight—bike won. Well... more like curb won." He shrugged again. "Doesn't even hurt."

Wren reached out and gently took his wrist in her hands. Brantley winced. "Doesn't hurt, huh?" Seeing the bruising went all the way around his wrist, her brow scrunched. *How could hitting a curb do that?* She wanted to ask him, but this time, restrained herself. "It's really swollen. Maybe Elisi has something—"

Brantley pulled back his hand. "No. Really." He tugged down his sleeve. "I'm good." He switched to his other hand and reached into his backpack, pulling out a rolled piece of paper. "Let's just get started, okay?"

Wren knew he was lying. The investigator gene in her gut made her want to press him. Made her want to find out who had hurt him. But that same gene told her if she did, she could end up setting the world record for Fastest Time to Lose a Friend, before she'd even officially become one. So, she told herself, she'd leave it alone. *For now.*

Elisi walked into the room with a tray loaded with enough food and drink to sustain a small scouting party. Ham and cheese piled high on homemade wheat bread, chips, and warm oatmeal cookies. She put the tray down on the dresser and handed Brantley a glass. "I hope you like lemonade. Fresh-squeezed."

Brantley wasn't shy. His eyes lit up as he grabbed a cookie. "This is great!" He swiped his hand across his partially full mouth and swallowed, "Sorry." He shrugged and gave her a slightly embarrassed smile. "Guess I was hungry."

"Nonsense." Elisi waved him off. "It's my cooking. It's so wonderful, you can't help yourself." She nodded at Wren. "Go ahead. Tell him."

Wren raised an eyebrow. "Oh yeah, Grandma, you're a regular Gordon Ramsay."

Elisi put her hands on her hips. "Pa-leeze, Gordon Ramsay wishes he could make my cookies."

Brantley grabbed another one, took a bite, then held up the rest of the cookie. "True that."

Wren and Elisi busted out laughing.

Brantley washed down the cookie with lemonade and sat the glass down on the tray. "How do you say *thank you* in Cherokee?"

Elisi's eyes brightened at his interest. "Wado." She smiled. "And you are most welcome."

"Wa-doh," Brantley said as he grabbed a sandwich. "How—"

Wren held up a hand up to stop him. "Trust me, you're not ready for *you're welcome*."

Elisi chuckled. "Probably right. Baby steps." She turned toward the door. "I'll leave you two detectives to it then." She pointed at Wren. "Remember, gathering information for Landry only. Nothing. Dangerous." Then she wagged her finger at both of them. "That goes for you too, mister, in any language."

"Yes, ma'am."

Wren gave a thumbs-up. "Got it."

Brantley finished his cookie and wiped his hand on his jeans. He looked over the already mostly taken-up whiteboard. "Hey, I've got an idea. Okay?"

She nodded.

He pulled all the reports off the board and spread them

out on the floor, then unrolled the paper he'd pulled from his backpack—a street map of Fort Gibson—and taped all four corners to the right side of the whiteboard. "First things first. We map out the scene of the crimes."

He dug around his backpack again and pulled out a handful of Sharpies. "Read me the addresses."

"Okay, I found J.R. shot…there…" She pointed to the field by Simpson's pasture. She didn't need a piece of paper for that one. Brantley made a red dot by her finger.

Wren picked up the reports, then looked at the map. "And the cat that was—"

Brantley held up his hand. "Look, it's not like I'm a wimp or anything—I'm not—okay—but animals…" He shook his head. "Sorry, I can't take the details. Just the address please."

She nodded. "No worries." Her eyes squinted as she searched for the right street on the map. "There…" She marked the spot with her finger. "Right off Cemetery Road."

Brantley nodded. "Got it," he said. Another red dot.

She gave him the addresses from the remaining reports, and he marked their locations.

Wren leafed through the reports in her hands. The papers that had all those gory details Brantley couldn't take. And it made her wonder…why could she? Was it all the crime shows she watched? Podcasts she listened to? The countless hours of Internet searching and graphic images that had burned themselves into her brain? Had they dulled her senses? Made her numb?

Or, maybe it was just a desire for justice—her drive to find the person responsible that outweighed everything. She scoffed. That sounded *exactly* like something a cop would say. Like her dad would say.

Brantley snapped his fingers and waved his hand in front of her face. "Earth to Wren. You okay?"

She shook her head. "Oh…sorry…"

"Where'd you go?"

"Nowhere, just—what's next?"

"I don't know…maybe add dates?"

Wren nodded and tried to regain her focus on the task at hand.

Shuffling the reports into date order, she grabbed the blue dry-erase marker she'd taken from Landry's desk and made a list—one-through-six—on the left side of the board, followed by the report's date.

Brantley added the number beside each corresponding dot on the map, drew a large kidney-shaped circle around them all, then tapped the circle. "Most perps stick to an area they feel comfortable with."

Wren shot him a sideward glance. Perps? Apparently, she wasn't the only one who watched and listened to true crime.

They sat back and admired their handiwork. Who knows? Her dad might even be impressed—if she was ever crazy enough to let him see it.

Although unsure of what to do next, at least their target area was defined, which, from her podcasts, she knew was the first step in detecting patterns. It made Wren's stomach all fluttery, knowing that odds were, whoever hurt these animals either lived or worked inside that red circle.

Brantley put the cap on the red Sharpie, stood, and after having two refills of lemonade, asked for the bathroom.

Wren pointed him in the direction without taking her eyes off the board. This time not seeing a taped map with dots and circles, but images of those poor animals and what they had gone through. *Who did this? Why?* Two more to add to the pile of questions she didn't have answers to. But, if she couldn't find her mom—the one answer she most desperately wanted—she promised herself that she would at least find the answer to the most important one of these two.

She picked up the reports again and held them in her hands. She blew out a long breath. Wren had never lied to her grandmother. Never broken a promise. Not even once.

"Sorry, Elisi," she whispered. "I will find who is doing this. And I will stop them. Dangerous or not."

Chapter Nineteen

Brantley had gone home, saying he couldn't be late. The cop's daughter in Wren noticed he ran his hand over his hurt wrist as he said it. Elisi was gathering her things and about to head out the door to Tahlequah to visit friends.

"Sure you won't come? Everyone would love to see you." Elisi jangled the truck keys to aid in the enticement—or maybe to show, for once, she didn't need Wren's help to find them.

Wren, still sitting cross-legged in front of the murder board, scrunched her face. "Nah, homework." She nodded toward the board. "And I want to see what I can figure out on this. Buuut... I wouldn't hate it if you brought me back some onion rings from Del Rancho. And—"

Elisi raised a hand to stop her. "A Dr Pepper with extra ice."

Wren rubbed her hands together. "They have the best ice."

Elisi nodded. "True that."

Wren fell back on the floor laughing.

Elisi blew her a kiss. "Okay then, I'm off. Probably best if homework came first before any figuring, don't you think?" she said with a smile, her question obviously rhetorical. "I won't be too late. I promise. I'll let you know when I'm heading back this way."

Wren nodded. They had gotten into an unspoken habit of letting each other know where they were, when they were headed home, and especially when they were running late. Periodic updates that said, *Relax, everything's okay—I'm okay. I'll be home soon.*

It was progress, though. For the longest time her dad and Elisi wouldn't let her go anywhere or be on her own. For the longest time, she hadn't wanted to.

She got up and double-checked the lock on the front door, refilled her lemonade, and went back to her room. She didn't really have homework, she just didn't feel like being a tagalong with Elisi and her friends tonight. Plus, this would give her some time alone to work on the board. She munched on half of a sandwich, stared at the board, and tried to conjure up some what-to-do-next inspiration.

"A good investigation requires good organization." She nodded, agreeing with herself. She'd learned that much from hanging around the police station. Cops were sticklers for details. Some, like her dad, lived for them. She put down her sandwich, wiped her hands off on her jeans, and grabbed the blue dry-erase marker, intending to add the owner's last name and the type of animal to their one-through-six list. For Brantley's sake, she would leave off any injury details. It was a stretch to think the owners would have something in common that would lead to anything, but in her dad's words: *A big part of investigations is the process of elimination.* She had only made it halfway through before the marker squeaked dry across the board.

She shook the marker, but it didn't help. "Crap!" She tossed it into the trash can beside her desk, mad at herself for not thinking it had probably sat in Landry's desk for at least as long as the whiteboard had sat in the storeroom. It was surprising it had worked at all. She sighed. Great, that was the only dry-erase marker she had. Now what?

The obvious answer? Her dad's office was surely well stocked. She bit on her bottom lip as she glanced down the hall. But…his home office was also off-limits.

She guessed she could hop on her bike and run down to the Dollar General. She checked the time and shook her head. It was already close to dark, and Elisi would kill her.

Or…she could have Elisi bring back some markers along with the onion rings and just wait to finish the board—maybe practice some of that patience thing Elisi was always encouraging.

Nope…This time, patience would have to wait. She needed to figure this out before some other poor animal got hurt—or worse.

She sneaked down the hardwood floors of the hallway as if she wasn't the only one there, feeling the chill of the evening seep through her socks. She stood in front of his office door and reached for the knob, then drew back her hand. This was uncharted territory. They had their issues, Wren and her dad, and although she'd made the truth bendable at times, she'd never out-and-out disobeyed him.

But this was an actual investigation, right? Crimes were being committed and she was on a mission to stop them. Surely, he of all people, could—would understand that.

She turned the knob, and crossed the threshold, as if it was an actual line she'd just crossed. It was crazy. Feeling so jittery. Like he could walk in any minute and catch her. For the luva Pete, it's a home office, she told herself, not CIA headquarters.

But he had made such a point of it…Why?

A windblown limb of the oak tree scratched back and forth across the window screen. Like a wagging finger, warning not to go farther. Retreat. Close the door behind you. Wipe the knob of all fingerprints. She swallowed hard, trying to push down the tingly feeling of committing what was akin to a family version of a first-degree felony. But...she was already inside, and the deed was already done. Might as well get what she came for.

She walked to his desk and tried the bottom drawers. Locked. She scoffed. *So much for trust.* She rolled back his chair and pulled out the center drawer and found neatly stacked bins of pens, pencils, binder clips, paper clips, and dry-erase markers. Jackpot! She wouldn't put it past her dad to have everything in the drawer categorized and inventoried, but that was another chance she would have to take.

As she pushed the drawer closed, something caught her eye. *What is that?* She pulled the drawer back open.

It was a fold of white tissue paper tucked off to the right side. A tiny pool of silver chain peeked out from the bottom. Her hand trembled as she reached for it, as she felt its weight in her hand. And she just knew.

Her mother's necklace.

The one that matched the necklace around Wren's neck.

The one her mother never—ever—took off.

She unwrapped the tissue paper slowly, not wanting it to tear, and laid the necklace out on the desktop. Her whole body smoldered with anger—confusion about what this meant.

She stared at the necklace—here was something tangible, something real to hold of her mom's. Not a hair clip or earrings she wore now and then. She wore this every single day since they'd gotten them.

Her stomach dropped. It was complicated with her dad, sure, but she had always trusted him, hadn't she?

She picked up the necklace and held it to her chest. Trying to absorb any iota of her mother's energy that might remain.

Horrible thoughts engulfed her. *Was this why he never wanted anyone in here? What else is here? Did he have something to do with her going missing?*

The air went out of her lungs, out of the room. And for a moment she was frozen. Numb.

She no longer cared about getting in trouble for invading his private space. He owed her answers, and they couldn't wait. She wouldn't wait.

She ran to her room and grabbed her phone. She needed to hear his voice—needed to know if he was telling her the truth. Or worse, hiding something more. She clicked on his name on her very short list of contacts and sent him an even shorter text:

CALL ME. 911.

Chapter Twenty

"What's wrong?" her dad asked the second she answered the phone. He sounded calm, but Wren could hear the tinges of panic in his voice.

"Wrenie? Are you there?"

She was cross-legged on her bed, the necklace and the framed picture from her bedside table in front of her. She'd sat there, waiting on his call, but now that he was on the phone, she couldn't respond, couldn't unmix the jumble of words and questions in her head.

"I found Mom's necklace," she finally blurted.

Silence.

"I know I'm not supposed to be in your office, but I needed—" Her voice hitched. "Why do you have Mom's necklace?" She wailed her words like the pain-filled cries of a wounded animal. She swiped at the hot tears that fell. "Why...," she cried.

More silence. She pulled the phone away to see if they were still connected. She pressed the phone back to her ear. "Daddy?"

"I—I'm so sorry you found it like that, Wrenie. I can't imagine..." His voice trailed off. He cleared his throat. "The turquoise was loose. Your mom had taken it in to get it repaired the week before—" He paused. She heard him blow out a shaky breath. "They called for it to be picked up after. It was selfish, I know.... I should've shown it to you and Elisi. Should've shared it with you. I... just... I guess I just wanted something of hers for myself. Can you understand that, Wrenie? Can you forgive me?"

Now the silence was hers. Of course she could understand. That's exactly why she clung so tightly to her own necklace. To her favorite picture beside her bed. And now to her red cord bracelet. She craved pieces—reminders of her mother anywhere she could find them.

"I'm sorry most of all, Wrenie, that I couldn't protect her.... And that I haven't been able to bring her back to us."

His words felt like a kill-punch to the solar plexus. How selfish—how stupid had she been to think, even for a second, he wasn't hurting just because she couldn't visibly see it? Could it be she'd been so tied up in her own loss that she hadn't really been looking? Or worse still... had she, without even realizing it, been blaming him too?

She fought to push down the lump in her throat. Just like her, just like Elisi, her dad was doing the best he could under these most horrible circumstances.

Her grasp tightened around the phone. The animosity, the anger, the five-plus years of frustrations that made up all those bricks in the wall between them crumbled. "I love you, Daddy," she said softly. "It's nobody's fault but the person who took her."

Chapter Twenty-One

Dragging herself out of bed, Wren did a quick inspection in the bathroom mirror and grimaced. She splashed handfuls of icy water on her face to shrink the puffiness from her eyes. An unattractive souvenir from her dad's phone calls. He'd called her again multiple times over the weekend to check on her. When all was said and done, they decided it best not to mention the necklace to Elisi. No sense in upsetting her. She'd cried over that, too. She hated keeping things from Elisi but finally agreed with her dad it was the best thing to do.

The cold water helped, but the stress hangover from finding the necklace and confronting her dad still made her feel like fresh roadkill. Thankfully, they were out of school for two whole days for teacher conferences, so Wren and Brantley were free to do as they pleased. Christmas in October. She needed it.

Brantley had come over early enough to partake of Elisi's Famous Cinnamon Waffles. She could hear him and Elisi in the kitchen. She'd better get dressed and get out there if she wanted some.

"Seconds anyone?" Wren heard Elisi ask as she sat down at the table.

Elisi slid another waffle onto Brantley's plate, already knowing the answer. Butter pooled in each little square, leaving no room for syrup, but Brantley reached for it anyway.

"Wado," he said with his mouth full.

Wren had to smile.

Brantley had a talent for showing up whenever food was about to hit the table. "Are you hungry?" Elisi would ask. "I could eat," he'd say with a shrug, but his face would light up like it was the best offer ever. It wasn't long before Elisi stopped asking. When the doorbell rang, she'd head straight for the kitchen.

Wren finished her waffles and her glass of milk and carried her dishes to the sink. Brantley did the same.

Elisi shooed them away. "You two go ahead. I've got this."

Brantley grabbed an extra piece of bacon off the plate by the stove as they headed toward Wren's room.

Wren showed him the updates she'd made on the murder board, then sat down on the floor. She shrugged. "Now what?"

Brantley nodded at the map. "You know, the target area's not all that big and it's not far." He pointed at the bottom of the red kidney-shaped circle. "My house is right there. Why don't we do a ride-by around the different locations and see if we spot anything suspicious?

Wren nodded. "Sounds good to me." She pulled her phone from her back pocket and snapped a picture of the board, so they'd have the addresses.

ᴏᴓᴏ

They biked past their first two stops off 2 Mile Road, but saw nothing. She looked at her phone. "Next is..."

"McDonald's," Brantley said more as a statement than an ask. "I could do with some fries."

Wren eyes widened. "Seriously? We just ate, like, two seconds ago."

Brantley gestured down at his bike. "Hello…we've been exercising."

Wren opened her mouth to give him more grief but decided fries and a Dr Pepper didn't sound half bad.

They hit McDonald's before the lunch rush, but it was still busy. Free days from school apparently required celebrating with a quarter pounder.

Wren had no more sat down at their table and stuck the end of a fry in her mouth before M.J. and her minions appeared, trays in hand. She breathed a sigh of relief when it looked as if M.J. hadn't noticed them as she walked past.

But M.J. circled back and came up behind her. "Why if it isn't Wren and her little boyfriend." She targeted her laser sight at Brantley. "Who are you, again?" she asked, just to make him feel insignificant in a town where everybody knows everybody from kindergarten to twelfth grade. She waved him off. "Doesn't matter. You're as forgettable as your freakazoid stalker brother."

Wren scrunched her brow. "Sooo…you know who his brother is, but you don't know who he is?"

M.J. ignored the call-out and pasted on her fake smile. "Oh, Wren…can I ask a favor?"

Wren sighed. She was so over M.J. and all her crap. She put a hand on her chest and pasted the most accommodating look she could muster on her face. "Sure, *Meagan*, whatever you need."

M.J.'s eyes narrowed and her face flushed red. Her minions took a step back, unsure what was coming next. M.J. scoffed—just a little one, but enough to let Wren know she'd scored a point.

M.J. tilted her head and smiled through her perfect clenched teeth and put her hand on Wren's shoulder. "I was wondering… I'm thinking of going as a Cherokee princess for Halloween and I need a headdress. Can I borrow one?" She cut her eyes to her minions as if signaling going for the jugular, then the fake-innocent look returned. "I mean, I'm sure your mom isn't using hers, right?"

Brantley jumped up, his chair scrapping against the floor. "YOU—"

M.J. stuck her hand up in front of his face, not about to listen.

All of McDonald's was watching the show.

Wren sat there frozen. Silent. Numb.

M.J. patted Wren's shoulder again. "Okay, then, just let me know if you can hook me up. I'd really appreciate it."

And just like that, her mission accomplished, M.J. and her entourage were gone.

Brantley sat back down. "I can't believe…What a…" He leaned toward Wren. "Are you okay?"

Wren nodded. But she wasn't. Not even close. Even knowing what an evil person M.J. was and what she was capable of, Wren never thought she'd go…there.

"That crossed WAY OVER the line," Brantley said. "Maybe you should, you know, tell somebody—report her to Principal Endicott. I'll go with you and back you up."

There it was. Proof. Wren did have a friend. Someone she could count on. It was official. And he was right. She should tell somebody. Not because she couldn't handle the likes of Meagan Jacobs, but because somebody else she picked on might not be able to.

But that could wait. The likes of Meagan Jacobs wasn't her priority.

Chapter Twenty-Two

Wren and Brantley dumped their fries and drinks in the trash, walked outside, and straddled their bikes.

"Feel like finishing the circle or do you just wanna go on home?" Brantley asked.

Wren rolled her eyes. "Pa-leeze. She may have got me for a minute, but I'm over it."

Brantley smiled, then swiped up his kickstand. "Okay! Follow me."

Instead, Wren took off first. "You follow me!" she threw over her shoulder.

They raced their way back toward 2 Mile Road, taking turns at the lead. After checking out a few more of the abuse sites and coming up empty, Brantley turned in to a gravel drive.

"What's left?" Brantley asked as Wren pulled up beside him.

Wren took out her phone and checked the picture of the murder board list. "I think...that's...pretty much all...except—"

Brantley stopped her. "The tortured cat."

She raised both hands. "I wasn't going to say anything."

Brantley shuddered. "Sorry, I'm out for that one. You can fill me in later. Just, no—you know."

Wren nodded. "I know. No details."

He tilted his head and smiled. "No clues, but pretty nice day anyway, right?

"Well, except for the run-in with Her Highness."

"Yeah…let's not do that again."

Wren laughed. "Agreed." It had been a nice day. In fact, she couldn't remember the last time she'd had so much fun.

Brantley laughed too, then nodded toward the other end of the long gravel drive, to a white two-story house with faded blue shutters and a detached garage that sat back off the road. "This is me. Wanna—" A front window curtain moved to the side. Brantley stood up off his bike. "Shoot." The color in his face drained. "Never mind. My dad's home. He wasn't—I gotta go." He pressed hard on his pedals, making the gravel crunch under his wheels.

Wren sat back on her bike and watched him. He dropped his bike in the front yard, tires still spinning, and hurried through the front door. Then it struck her. The bike drop, the barging in the house, was just like she'd done hundreds, if not thousands, of times. But she had Elisi there to greet her. A hug, a smile, a taste test of whatever she had on the stove, that, no matter what kind of day she'd had, automatically filled Wren with the warmth of knowing she was loved. A feeling she could now see wasn't something to be taken for granted. And it made her wonder, *What was waiting for Brantley, behind his front door?*

She had to do something. She wasn't sure what, but as she steered her bike back onto the street toward the last crime scene, she *was* sure of one thing. He deserved better.

◦ ✇ ◦

Wren wheeled up to the section of chain-link fence where Landry had found the cat's body. It was doubtful she'd find anything at this location either, but in any investigation, it was important to be thorough. (Ask her how many times she's overheard her dad say that to one of his officers).

She looked around the area and wondered what else she should do. She could go door-to-door and ask neighbors if they saw something, but that might get back to Landry and her dad. Besides, if somebody saw someone hurting an animal, she had to believe they would've stopped it and reported it. She sure didn't want to believe otherwise.

She walked over to the fence and put her back against it—taking the vantage point of the poor cat—and looked around for anything helpful. Suddenly, her breath caught. How had she not noticed? Coming this way from Brantley's house, nothing had looked familiar. But now she knew exactly where she was. There, across the street on the corner, was the back of a house she'd been to many, many times before. A house whose owner was so thankful to Wren for saving little J.R.'s life that she'd be happy to answer any questions. Happy to help find who shot J.R. any way she could.

But then, as she made her way across the street and got closer to the house, Wren's heart began to race, and a wide grin spread across her face. Mounted on the corner eaves of Susan's house was the most beautiful thing Wren had ever seen.

Security cameras.

Chapter Twenty-Three

Susan answered the door looking much more put together than the last time Wren had seen her. She had J.R. cradled in one arm and opened the screen with the other.

"Wren! We're so happy to see you! Please come in."

Wren scratched between J.R.'s ears. "Hey there, big guy. How ya doing?"

Susan turned so Wren could see his tail giving her side forty lashes and laughed. "There's your answer."

Wren followed them into the living room. As soon as they sat down on the sofa, J.R. wrestled free from Susan's arms, hobbled over to Wren's lap, and proceeded to give her face a thousand kisses.

"Looks like somebody's grateful." Susan chuckled. "That makes two of us. Let me get my checkbook."

Wren was giggling. "I think I've just been paid in full."

Suddenly worn out from the display of gratitude, J.R. plopped down on the sofa beside her. His little body was warm against Wren's thigh. His makeshift protective collar, made from a bright blue pool noodle, propped his head up like a travel pillow. Wren stroked him softly and he closed his eyes.

Susan came back into the room, checkbook in hand. "He

hated the ridiculous plastic cone Doc Foley gave me." She nodded toward the noodle collar and smiled. "So, I YouTubed it. Do you have any idea how hard it is to find a pool noodle in October?" She laughed again. "Guess I should've hired you for that, too."

She sat back down on the edge of the sofa and leaned over her checkbook.

Wren held up her hands. "No, Ms.—Susan, please. You don't owe me anything, really."

Susan kept writing. "Nonsense. I owe you everything. You saved my J.R.'s life and brought him back to me." She tore out the check and handed it to Wren. "I only wish I could give more."

Let people reward you for making their hearts whole again, Elisi's words replayed in her head. So she smiled, took the check, and slipped it into her jacket pocket without looking at the amount. "Thank you," Wren said, and went back to petting J.R. "This little guy is like family to me, too."

Susan smiled. "Can I get you something to drink? Some hot chocolate, maybe? It's getting chilly out there. I have pumpkin spice."

"Great, thanks!" Wren stood up to follow her into the kitchen. J.R. popped one eye open, then was out again.

Wren held on to the edge of the kitchen counter to help muster her courage as Susan fussed with mugs and boiling water. Wren blew out a breath and went for it. "Susan…can I ask a favor?"

Wren always had a flash drive on her key ring for school, but since Elisi was going to be home all day, she'd left her keys. The plan, after Susan had responded with an eager, *Anything you want*, and they were sipping their pumpkin spice cocoa, was to email the video from Susan's security cameras to herself. If she named the file something like: *Cramp Remedies*, her dad wouldn't go near it. But she hadn't considered how humongous the file was. Emailing was out of the question.

Susan hadn't been any help. "Sorry, hon. I don't have a clue." She waved toward the computer. "My brother set all that up. Me? I'm lucky to work the TV remote."

Wren's shoulders sagged. She couldn't ask Susan to let her sit here and go through hours of video coverage. It was already late in the day, and she needed to head home. Elisi would be watching for her. She wanted the footage now, but the universe was forcing her to wait. Forcing her to pause, regroup, and think about what she should do.

Patience. Ugh.

Wren tried to mask the disappointment all over her face. "Thanks anyway. If I can figure out how to do it, I'll come back later, if it's okay?"

Susan nodded as Wren went over to the still sleeping J.R. and gently ran her hand down his side. "Feel better, buddy," she whispered.

Susan, who looked just as disappointed, walked Wren to the door. "I'm sorry...I wish—wait!" Her eyes flew open wide. "I don't know why I didn't think of it sooner." She grabbed Wren's hand. "Stay right here."

She came back, waving what looked like a business card in her hand. "I totally forgot because I could never figure it out, but my brother set it up so I could access the cameras on my phone and check on J.R. while I'm at work." She showed Wren the card. "Couldn't you do that, too?"

Wren took the card and couldn't believe her eyes. The security company's logo and website on the front—account login and password on the back. Everything she needed. Duh! Why hadn't *she* thought of it sooner? Not that she had any experience with security system apps, but *everything* was cloud based now. Wren threw her arms around Susan and hugged her. "Yes!" she squealed, "Thank you!" Her hand flew to her mouth, not meaning to be so loud. J.R. raised his head, then plopped back down, disinterested. "Thank you," she said again, this time in a whisper.

The second Susan's front door shut behind her, Wren pulled out her phone and texted Brantley. She jumped onto her bike and rode home fast, with a smile so big, her teeth would've caught every bug in three counties had it been June instead of October. In her possession was access to a real, honest-to-God clue that might bust this case wide open, and she couldn't wait to see it—couldn't wait for Brantley to see it with her. She pedaled faster.

The sky was gray, and the air had that earthy smell that signals rain. The temperature had dropped while she'd been visiting with Susan and J.R., but the cold had no effect. The pink in her cheeks, the white knuckles on the handlebars, weren't from the cold or the aerobics of a brisk ride. It was solely, 100 percent pure excitement. Sure, she had been determined to help Landry stop the abuse and bust the creep doing it, but somewhere in the back of her mind was a tiny little voice that kept telling her, *You're just a kid. What can you do?* A voice that sounded just like her and made her feel worthless. And feeling that way sucked.

But I'm not worthless, Wren would argue with herself. She was good at investigating. Good at this finding thing. Maybe, if she and Brantley could solve this case, it might be just the beginning. A way to make a difference. And maybe a way to tell that voice, *Shut up.*

She dropped her bike in the yard and bounded through the front door, her eyes on her phone the whole way. Nothing from Brantley. She started toward her bedroom.

"Door!" Elisi yelled from the kitchen. "We're not heating the whole neighborhood!"

Wren wheeled around and kicked the door shut, a little harder than she'd intended. "Sorry," she muttered, her head buried in her phone as she passed by the kitchen. Her thumbs punched out:

U THERE?

She stared at the screen all the way to her bedroom, as if her laser-locked gaze might make Brantley drop whatever he was doing, pick up his phone, and respond. She sat down at her desk almost missing the chair. Still, nothing.

She heard the faint ring of the landline and Elisi pick it up in the kitchen, but she paid it no mind. "ARGH!" she yelled at her phone "TEXT ME!" She tossed it onto the desk.

She chewed on her lip and wrapped her feet around the legs of the chair to keep them from bouncing. She was dying to review the video, but she should wait, shouldn't she? It didn't seem fair to do it without him. He was her partner.

It had only been minutes since she'd sent her last text to Brantley, but it felt more like hours. She couldn't stand it anymore. Besides, the more she thought about it, he hadn't wanted to hear the details of the abuse from the reports. If the video did manage to capture something, no way he could handle actually seeing it.

She dug the login card out of her back pocket, opened her laptop, and typed in the security company's website. Under customer login, she entered Susan's username and password, and let the little processing circle get to work.

A live camera grid popped up on her screen. Two on the front of the house, two on the back, and what looked like a view from the storage shed in the back that covered most of both sides. She looked at them closely. It wasn't a perfect shot, and it was some distance away, but the best view to where Landry found the cat, was rear-camera-left angle.

She had her camera, now all she needed to find was the right file.

It took her a minute, but she was able to dig around and find the archived recordings. It was a long list of files, named after the camera and the date of the recording. Her stomach got all quivery as her cursor hovered over the video file for the day Landry found the cat. Her pointer finger was suddenly reluctant to double-click. This wasn't some made-for-TV movie or fake cop show. She had a stronger stomach than Brantley, for sure, but the possibility of watching a video of a real murder that happened right here in Fort Gibson? She wasn't totally sure she could handle seeing that either.

She blew out a long breath and steeled herself. If she thought, even for a second, that she might really consider being a cop, a detective, a private investigator, she'd have to be able to handle things like this—and worse. She hit play.

"Wrenie, could you come out here, please? Now." Her dad's voice coming from outside her bedroom door startled her. He wasn't supposed to be home for two more days. She'd left the board out. Had he found out what she had been up to? Her stomach seized. She slammed the laptop shut and shoved the murder board under her bed.

She hurried to the living room to find her dad standing in the middle of the room. He had a strange look on his face. Elisi was sitting on the sofa, so pale she looked Caucasian, nervously kneading the dish towel in her hands.

"Dad, I can ex—"

"Wrenie," he interrupted. "Come, sit down. I've got something to tell you."

She sat down next to Elisi, who released her grip on the towel and grabbed Wren's hand.

Wren's breath caught. Her dark brown eyes grew wide. "What's going on? What's wrong?" Her voice went shrill. "Dad, you're scaring me."

Her dad sat on the arm of the sofa beside her and took her other hand in his. Wren could see he was fighting to keep his composure. He shook his head. "I don't—" He paused, looked down, then found her eyes again. His breath hitched. "Some remains have been found, Wrenie," he said softly. "Nothing is for sure...but there's a chance it could be Mom."

She yanked her hands away. They flew up to her ears as if she could stop his words from getting in. "NO!" she cried, searching his face, Elisi's face, for any sign this was a mistake.

He slid down on the sofa to hug her, but she sprung to her feet and whirled around to face Elisi.

"Grandma?" came out as a whimper. Then Wren saw it. Elisi's strong, vibrant, eyes had been watered down into dull brown waves full of pain. Her father had gone and broken her sweet Elisi with his brutal words.

Her breath caught. Her heart pounded.

This was real.

This was happening.

The room spun around her. She dropped to her knees. Dizzy, so, so dizzy. Her stomach revolted.

Her dad kneeled beside her and held back her hair. "I'm sorry, baby," he kept saying in between her dry heaves, "I'm so very sorry."

Chapter Twenty-Four

The world looked different now. The bright fall leaves—the holdouts that still clung to the trees—seemed dulled and withered. Food, Elisi's Famous or not, fell flat on her tongue. The tiger pawprints painted on the street leading the way to school were now just something to ride her bike over.

Wren hadn't wanted to go back to school. Didn't want to do anything but sit and wait for the phone to ring. Wait for the call that would give them a definitive answer. But they made her go, Elisi and her dad, saying utterly ridiculous things like, "Your schoolwork will keep you busy," and "It'll help keep your mind off things."

Yeah. Right.

After all her screaming, crying, and dry heaving was over, her whole body went numb. As if every ounce of hope she'd been holding on to all these years had been instantly drained from her. As if, by his words, her father had pulled her faith plug.

She steered her bike and the shell of herself down Ross Street, directly in front of a car. The driver slammed on his brakes, blared his horn, and yelled something not-so-nice out the window. But Wren didn't care, almost wishing he would've hit her.

The whole ride, all she did care about was replaying every word her dad had said.

"The remains were found outside my jurisdiction," he said as gently as one could say such a horrible thing. "They're being sent to the state for further examination." He put his hand on her shoulder. "Wrenie, I know it's hard, but we must be patient. It could take weeks, if not more, to get a proper identification. But there may be some media on this, so I thought you both should know."

He did say, *could be Mom*, not *is Mom*. So that was something. But him sitting her down and actually volunteering information? That told her something, too. He was being more forthcoming like they had begged him, but what had made her so very sick to her stomach was the feeling that what he was really doing was preparing them.

A blast of guilt hit her. Like the cold morning air hitting her face, it stung. She had wanted an answer. For as long as she could remember—more than anything. She'd get on her computer and search for one. Look to the stars and wish for one. Go to church every Sunday and pray for one. But she didn't want *this* to be the answer. She tightened her grip on the handlebars as her eyes blurred with tears. No matter what anyone said or how they said it, she wasn't—couldn't be prepared. Today, tomorrow, the next day . . .

She would *never* be ready to hear her mother was dead.

Chapter Twenty-Five

She walked into school and went straight for her locker, navigating the halls by following the seams in the linoleum. Even with her head down, she could feel their eyes, sense their whispers. It had been days since the as-of-yet-unidentified remains had been found and it had been all over the news. Not because of who it might be, but to reassure the listening audience it wasn't the fair-skinned girl everybody in the world was still out looking for.

Just last night the reporter had looked all serious as he read off the prompter. ". . . But preliminary results indicate the remains are Native American, female, approximately twenty to forty-five years of age. Official cause of death has not been released, but preliminary indications do point to foul play."

Wren had bristled as her research on MMIWG kicked in. "Big scoop there, Mr. Anchorman," she muttered. "That narrows it down to one of the thousands of our missing."

She had turned off the TV, and for the longest time, she sat there alone. Digesting. Trying to figure out how to feel something other than fearful...other than empty. Surprised she could feel them both at the same time. She remembered, once she'd overheard Elisi on the phone tell her friend we lived in limbo. Every day spent waiting for answers. Wren had gone straight to her bedroom and looked it up: *A state of uncertainty.* Yep…Elisi was right; for the last five years, their lives have been nothing but questions.

And now, ready or not, it looked like an answer was coming. If limbo had a cliff, Wren's toes were hanging over the edge of it.

But then she spotted her mom's crooked basket. On the shelf behind her, its reflection stared back at her in the TV's blank screen. It made her smile. And she decided to take it as a sign. A subtle nudge from the spirits, telling her, even now, to believe.

She sat up straighter and told herself, *Besides, if it was Mom, I would know.*

She would feel it. Maybe not with her finder feelings, but deep in her soul. In that unbreakable mother-daughter connection.

So…it wasn't her mom.

And if that meant a severe case of denial, so be it. For it was the only option that allowed her to continue to breathe. To put one foot in front of the other and go back to school—to the big fat Fort Gibson rumor mill.

"There are no secrets in a small town," Elisi reminded her at breakfast. "Whether they're true or not. Once sparked, they spread like wildfire. Pay them no mind, Usdi." Elisi, apparently, was choosing the denial route too.

There's no secrets in middle school either.

"Psst…did you hear?"

"Here she comes."

"You ask her…"

Trying her best to follow Elisi's advice, she rummaged through her locker—one book out…another in—careful to keep her eyes straight ahead. A big part of being successful at

122

denial is staying away from anything and anyone that could burst her protective bubble. Above all else, no sympathy. It's not like any of these people were her friends or really cared anyway. They were just drawn to drama like middle school moths to a flame.

She slammed the locker shut and headed to North Ed. No sooner had she walked into the building than there, standing right in front of her, was M.J., sans minions, but with her standard this-is-going-to-be fun look on her face.

Wren's blood pressure shot up so fast it made her face flush. She stepped toward M.J. and jabbed her finger into her face. "Say it," Wren hissed, and stepped even closer, backing M.J. against the wall. Hall traffic screeched to a halt.

M.J. was a full head taller than Wren, but she didn't care. She had been taking M.J.'s crap since third grade and pent-up rage was a great equalizer. "Go on...say ANYTHING about my mother." She narrowed her eyes. "I don't care who you think you are, or that my dad works for your dad. Say one word and I swear you'll regret it."

M.J. clutched her notebook tight to her chest as if it was a spiral-bound shield. Her eyes darted back and forth at their audience. She stood there, slack-jawed, like Wren had slapped the ability to speak right out of her.

Wren caught a glimpse of Coach Jackson heading their way. She took a step back, but continued giving M.J. a death stare.

Coach walked up beside them. "Everything okay here?" he asked, his eyebrows raised.

Wren nodded. M.J. did the same.

Coach Jackson eyed them both for a moment. "Good. See that it stays that way." As if considering the situation handled,

123

he glanced at his watch and headed back down the hallway, pointing at students along the way and barking, "Get to class."

Wren turned away from the still speechless M.J., slung her backpack over her shoulder, and strolled on to class, the hallways parting like the Red Sea. Feeling 100 percent like a Cherokee badass, she opened the classroom door, fighting the corners of her mouth from breaking into a full-blown smile. *That* was long overdue and the best she'd felt in a long time.

Brantley accosted her the second she plopped down in her seat. "Hey, I've been texting you." He sat down at the still empty desk beside her. "I heard."

Geez, she knew gossip traveled fast around here, but even she was shocked he'd already heard what she'd just done. Standing up to M.J. must be *really* big news.

"I'm sorry," he said, his face full of concern.

And then she knew. Wren looked at him and said nothing.

Brantley waited for a moment, then shrugged. "Uh... oh-kay...I just wanted to—"

"Don't."

"Don't what?"

"Don't say you're sorry. Because it's not her."

His concern morphed into confusion.

She splayed her hands on her desk. "Look...I just know it, okay. It's not her. It's not my mom. I don't need you to be sorry." She paused. "I need you to believe it with me."

Brantley eased himself back into the chair. He tilted his head and looked at her. She had no idea what he was thinking, but *Great, she's lost it* was a good guess.

The start of class bell rang, and the room broke into chaos. Mad dashes to the correct desk, the stashing of phones, backpacks dropping to the floor. Mrs. Myers laser-locked on the door to catch any stragglers.

"Brantley," Mrs. Myers said, never taking her eyes off the door. "To your seat, please." *How does she do that?*

But before he left, the corner of Brantley's mouth broke into a crooked little smile. And he simply said, "Done."

Wren smiled back in appreciation. But it wasn't until after he'd headed back to his desk that it registered why Brantley's smile had looked crooked.

Wren snuck her phone out of her backpack and saw all the missed messages Brantley had sent her. Friends checking on friends. She started to text him, then decided it was better to wait until after class and talk to him face-to-face. Make that face...to busted lip.

Chapter Twenty-Six

The days dragged. Still, no official results from the coroner's office. And definitely no talk of it at home. The few times her dad had broached the subject, Wren would jump up, stomp out of the room, and yell at the top of her lungs, "IT'S NOT HER!" before slamming her bedroom door.

A few minutes would pass, and from the other side of her door she'd hear Elisi's voice.

"I love you, Usdi. Danigtvlesdani."

Get through together. It was one of the first Cherokee phrases Elisi had taught her. And she'd been by Wren's side ever since.

The door-slamming, yelling meltdowns didn't happen often, but the potential was always there. Making the whole house feel tense, like an overstretched rubber band that could snap any moment. Elisi's now constant use of cedar smoke, since the remains had been found, could no longer be swept away by the wave of a hand or an opened window, having seeped into the pores of the walls. If it bothered her dad, Wren never heard him mention it.

She always felt bad after lashing out, but she couldn't help herself. It was like she went straight to DEFCON ONE. She simply couldn't bear to hear even a single syllable that sounded like their search for her mom was over. As if the act of allowing any such word to go from her ear to her brain would make it come true. Those remains were NOT her mom. They just couldn't be.

Her dad knocked on her door. Permission to enter wasn't granted, but he still cracked the door. "Sorry, Wrenie, I've got an emergency. I'll be back soon." He paused for a moment and when she said nothing, he retreated. "I love you," he said softly as he closed the door.

She listened for her dad's car to pull out of the driveway before coming out of her bedroom. She sat down on the sofa beside Elisi, who was all wrapped up in a live news report about a terrible stable fire off 3 Mile Road—not too far from their house. She laid her head on Elisi's shoulder, took in the faint flowery remnants of her lavender soap, and instantly felt better. Calmer.

Wren started to watch the broadcast too. Horrified, she pulled up her knees as earlier footage played of firefighters strong-arming hoses, directing torrents of water onto angry orange flames. Black smoke swirled all around them. Wren's hands covered her ears to muffle the sickening bleats and snorts of animals too scared to escape. Finally, the stable collapsed into a molten heap that nothing, or no one, could've survived. Wren's heart sank.

Elisi kept shaking her head.

The station switched back to live coverage as the fire chief stepped up to speak to the cameras. Firefighters continued to work behind him to ensure what little was left didn't reignite. It was a total loss.

"At approximately four thirty this afternoon," Chief Lunow announced, *"crews were notified of a possible structure fire involving a stable at this location. Crews arrived to find heavy fire conditions in the structure. It was unknown at the time if*

any persons were still inside. A primary search was conducted before crews were forced to retreat due to worsening conditions. During the search, several animals were rescued. At this time all persons have been accounted for, however, it is believed that two horses died in the rapidly progressing fire. The cause of the fire is currently under investigation. More information will be released when available."

The camera shot widened. Wren saw Landry's truck and her dad's car in the background. Suspected arson was all-hands-on-deck. Wren slipped her phone from her back pocket, selected her dad's number, and sent him a single heart emoji. Her apology.

Elisi patted Wren's leg. "You didn't get to finish your dinner. Are you hungry?"

Wren shook her head, kissed Elisi's cheek, and stood up. "Nah, thanks. Think I'll go on to bed. Being a raging nutjob is exhausting."

Elisi chuckled, but not her full-of-life laugh Wren loved to hear, which told Wren her grandmother was tired of the whole situation, too. "All right then, dear…see you in the morning."

A shadow of guilt and sadness crept over Wren's heart. She kept forgetting this whole nightmare wasn't all about her. Elisi had lost her daughter. Her dad had lost his wife. And Wren, acting like a jerk, had done nothing but hurt them more. She vowed on the way to her bedroom to do better. To remember.

She changed into her navy fleece pajama bottoms with bright pink stars and a white thermal T-shirt, then went to the bathroom to brush her teeth. She hurried across the cold floor in her bare feet, stubbing her toe on the edge of the murder board she'd slid under her bed.

She clutched her foot, fell back on her bed, and seriously considered the use of some really bad language. Probably karma for the way she'd acted earlier, but also a sign.

When the pain finally subsided to a dull throb, she went over to her desk, picked her phone off the charger, and sent Brantley a text—a shorthand version of tomorrow, after school, Operation Find-the-Animal-Killer-Jerkwad would recommence.

Chapter Twenty-Seven

The knock on her bedroom door jolted her awake. "Time to get up, Usdi. Breakfast won't eat itself."

Wren shut her eyes and tried to ignore the smell of sizzling bacon. She wanted desperately to go back to sleep. Back to the dream where her mother was *here...* in this very room... braiding Wren's hair for her first day of kindergarten.

She had rested her hands on Wren's shoulders and looked at her in the mirror. "Don't worry. It's easy. All you have to do is find someone by themselves who looks as scared on the outside as you feel on the inside. Go over to them. Smile and tell them your name. Make them feel better, and you'll make your first friend." She gave Wren a squeeze. "Guaranteed."

Then, like dreams do, they were whisked somewhere else with no explanation. Sitting in a booth at Charlie's Chicken, pretending to fight over the last corn nugget. Weird. She knew it was a dream while she was dreaming it—actually told herself, "This is a dream." It was like she was an observer standing in the wings watching their own story. Even weirder, when the dream version of herself giggled and popped that last priceless nugget into her mouth, Wren could taste the warm creamy corn as it coated her actual tongue.

And she was whisked away again, to snippets of three generations of memories she'd only seen in photos.... Elisi holding Wren's mom as a baby. Her mom laughing, enjoying a stomp dance, resting her hands on her about-to-pop belly. And lastly, Wren, in her mother's arms, just minutes after she was born.

The warmth of the dream, of her mother's smile, seeped into every cell of her body, into the marrow of her bones, as if while lying there, she was draped with a heavy Native blanket, hung out on the line, and dried all day in the sun. A warmth she never wanted to end.

She fought waking. Each time her head peeked above the surface of dreamland, the harder it was to hit replay again. As hard as she tried, as much as she wanted to, she couldn't keep the dream from growing more and more hazy—couldn't keep it from slipping out of reach.

Finally, it was the smell of bacon that proved too much. She trudged into the kitchen, her shoulders droopy, her arms hung loose at her sides. She tilted her head back and, in a fake-whiney voice said, "Need. Energy. Need. Coffee."

"Caffeine stunts your growth," Elisi said, paying her no attention, making her a plate.

Wren shuffled her fuzzy footies back to her room and brought back her phone. "Hey, Google. Does coffee really stunt your growth?"

She plodded over to Elisi, eyes still half closed, and held the phone up.

"There is no concrete evidence that links coffee consumption and a person's growth . . ."

Wren shrugged. "If the Google lady says it . . ."

Elisi rolled her eyes, shook her head, then ceded. "Fine. What do I care if you need a booster seat for the rest of your life." She pulled a mug out of the cupboard, poured Wren half a cup, and set it down in front of her. She raised a finger. "Consumer warning: Your dad likes it strong as mud, so you might end up short AND with hair on your chest."

Wren stifled a laugh, looked down at the mostly flat front of her shirt, and drew an air circle around her chest. "Anything that adds to this particular area would be most welcome."

They laughed. For whatever reason, the energy in the house seemed more relaxed now—more back to normal. And it occurred to Wren that she had been the one responsible for most of the tension. Maybe making the decision to try to do better was making a difference already.

◌◌◌

Between classes, she walked up on Brantley and touched him on the shoulder.

He backed his head out of his locker and tossed his bangs out of his eyes. It had been sweater weather yesterday but today, they both were in T-shirts. Brantley had ventured all the way back into shorts, but to Wren, that was carrying things a little too far. It *was* still October.

He smiled.

His lip had mostly healed, and his smile was back to its stellar self, but if you were looking—and she was—you could still see traces. She had been proud of herself at the time. Even with the stuff about her mom going on, she'd remembered to ask him about it, getting some bogus story about another epic bike crash. She scoffed. But *nobody's that* big of a klutz. What should she do? She felt trapped between wanting to help him and being afraid of losing her friend. The word *chicken* came to mind.

But she didn't want to take that on right now. Couldn't face it. So, she just smiled back. "Hey, okay if we go by the shelter first? With everything—" She waved it off. "Anyway, I haven't been around there much, plus I want you to meet Landry." Her mouth curled into a hint of a conniving grin. "You can distract him while I snoop around and take pictures of any new reports."

Brantley laughed. "Oh really? And how exactly am I supposed to distract him?"

"I don't know, you'll think of something. Besides...there are dogs," she said in a singsong way. "Big dogs, little dogs, puppies, cute little kittens. Might even be a pig or a horse if we're lucky."

"Okay, okay. I'm in. I'm in." He slammed his locker shut and leaned toward her. "You had me at big dogs."

She chuckled. "Good to know. Meet you at the bikes after."

❍❂❍

Landry was sitting at his desk doing paperwork when the two of them walked in. He looked up, a broad smile spread across his face. "Well, look what the cat dragged in...." He jumped up, came around the desk, and gave her a quick hug, then looked over at Brantley. "I guess that makes you the cat?"

Wren smiled. "This is Brantley. He's my friend from school." The word *friend* sort of caught in her throat as soon as she said it.

Brantley held out his hand. "Nice to meet you, sir."

Impressed, Landry raised his brow. "Sir, huh . . ." He looked over at Wren. "I like this guy." He turned back to Brantley and took his hand, giving it a healthy shake. He motioned them to come on in and pointed at the extra chairs. "Cop a squat," he said, going back around his desk to sit down. He grinned. "See, that's funny because I work for the police department."

Wren looked over at Brantley and rolled her eyes. "He thinks he's funny."

Landry leaned back in his chair and crossed his arms. "Darlin'...I know I am."

Wren smiled, but then faltered. "Sorry I haven't been around to help much lately. It's just—"

Landry waved his hand and leaned forward, his forearms on his desk. His face was full of compassion. "I heard, kiddo. I'm so sorry. Anything I can do?"

Wren shook her head. "No," she said firmly. "I-I mean, I don't really want to talk about it if that's okay. Besides, I don't believe it's her."

"*We* don't believe it's her," Brantley interjected.

A smile crept back onto Wren's face.

Landry pondered what they'd said for a moment and nodded.

"So...," Wren said, changing the subject. "What's new around here? I told Brantley about that terrible murdered cat you found. Please tell me you haven't had any more trouble."

Landry grimaced. "No, not like that, thank God. But I did find another dog that—"

Brantley's eyes widened as he held up his hands. "NO DETAILS!" he said a little too loudly, then composed himself. "Sorry...just... that cat . . ." He shook his head. "I can't take the details."

Landry nodded. "Understood. But this one wasn't tortured at least. Found the little guy over behind the Baptist church. He'd been shot." He looked over at Wren. "Afraid he wasn't as lucky as your friend J.R."

Wren's face fell.

"That's so mean," Brantley said. "Why?"

"Son, that's the million-dollar question."

"Know whose dog it was?" Brantley asked. "I mean, the owners must be so sad."

"No collar. Wasn't chipped. And nobody's called about him missing. Which makes it doubly sad when you think about it." Landry shook his head. "I don't know yet what's going on with all this, but with Halloween coming up, I gotta say I'm worried."

Wren nodded. Her time volunteering at the shelter had taught her Halloween could spell trouble for animals—particularly black cats.

"Which church?" Brantley asked, steering the conversation back to the latest dog that was shot. "The one on Jackson Street? My mom used to go there."

"Nope. First Free Will. At the end of Poplar."

"Wow, that's really terrible." Brantley nodded thoughtfully. "When did you find him?"

"Thursday afternoon. Another anonymous tip—" Landry shot Brantley a quizzical look, then chuckled. "Dude, I thought you weren't into details."

Brantley's cheeks flushed pink like he'd been caught with his hand in the cookie jar. He let out a nervous little laugh. "Oh, uh… sorry." He shrugged. "I mean, I like details—just not the gory kind."

Landry nodded. "Noted."

It took a minute, but Wren suppressed a grin, realizing

Brantley had gotten them everything they needed for their murder board without her having to snoop around.

Landry cocked his ear as sirens blared down Hickory Avenue. Every dog in the shelter joined in, howling backup in canine harmony. Seconds later, Landry's phone went off. His brow furrowed as he glanced at the screen. "Gotta run, guys. Duty calls."

Brantley stood up to let Landry get by.

Wren stood too. "We'll double-check the kennels and make sure everybody's good."

Landry picked up his bag. "Thanks, kiddo. But don't stay too long. Looks like it's trying to kick up a storm." He raised his hand as he walked out the door. "Nice meeting you, Brantley."

"You too," Brantley said, but Landry was already gone.

Wren showed Brantley the ropes. They tag-teamed the kennels, filling water bowls and doling out ear scratches and belly rubs, when three loud tones went off on her phone, followed by a voice familiar to anyone who's ever lived in Oklahoma:

"The National Weather Service has issued a tornado watch for the following counties in Oklahoma...."

She held her phone out front so they could both hear.

"...Wagoner...Muskogee...Cherokee..."

All around where they were standing.

They hurried to the front of the shelter and looked out the door. The sky had gone dark gray in the short time they'd been there. A menacing-looking wall cloud cut a line across the sky. They walked outside into air that was warm and sticky.

"We'd better go," Wren said as they hurried to their bikes.

Not that she was scared. Having lived her whole life in the part of the country called Tornado Alley, Wren knew what to do. It was ingrained in her DNA like a vaccination given at birth. She and Elisi had joked about it many times, imagining a baby popping out of the womb and the doctor telling the nurse, *"Shoot her up with—"*

"The tornado trifecta, Doctor?"

"Yes, yes... you know the drill...

1. *Seek shelter in a basement or a small inside room on the lowest floor.*
2. *Avoid windows, underpasses, vehicles.*
3. *Get under something sturdy or cover yourself with a mattress or blanket."*

The doctor would then whack the baby on the butt and say, *"Welcome to Oklahoma."*

So, knowing what to do and how to protect herself, tornadoes didn't really frighten her. In fact, she loved a good storm. Not the damage or anybody getting hurt, but the awe of what Mother Nature or Unelanvhi—the Creator, as Elisi would say—could stir up. It was a respect thing.

"I'd better get home," Brantley said. "You good?"

Wren nodded. "We've got a storm cellar in our backyard. There's plenty of room. Sure you don't want to come?"

He shook his head. "Nah, I'll be okay. Text ya later. Be safe."

"Okay," she said, a little worried that he had a lot farther to go than she did. But most of the time, these watches turned into nothing. "You be safe," she said anyway.

Her phone alerted her of a voicemail.

"Where are you?" Elisi's message said, the nervousness apparent in her voice. "Come home now."

She pushed the microphone icon and sent back a voice text,

not wanting to take the time to call. "Leaving shelter now. Be home soon." She tucked her phone back into her pocket.

She pedaled fast down the streets toward home. Past people out on their porches and lawns with their heads tilted back and their eyes looking skyward. When the weatherman says, *Seek shelter immediately*, most people in Oklahoma hear, *Go outside.*

She'd almost made it home when she felt the air change. The wind died and everything went electric. The tiny hairs on her arms and the back of her neck stood on end.

A wave of fear washed over her, feeling suddenly exposed. Feeling foolish for being out in the open.

The three loud tones on her phone sounded off again. No time to listen. Nothing to do but lean over the handlebars and pedal faster.

She jumped off her bike and let it crash in the yard as she ran toward the house.

Elisi, standing at the front door, watching for her, held out her hand. "Hurry, Usdi! Hurry!"

The tornado sirens blasted, sounding the alarm, as they hurried into the backyard and into the cellar. The vise in Wren's stomach tightened, knowing her dad had to stay out on duty in case of an emergency. But she desperately wanted him here. At home.

She stopped, just before shutting the cellar door. "I'll be right back," she said, bolting before Elisi could argue, and ran back into the house as fast as she could. The sirens blaring. The roar of the winds rising. Wanting, with everything in her, to rescue the prized framed photo of Wren and her mom from the table beside her bed. Mad at herself that she didn't have a copy of it on her phone.

She was running out of time though, she could feel it. Every fiber in her body screamed at her. RUN! But not toward the picture. She had one chance to save something, and it had to be special. She ran down the hallway and practically busted down the office door. She flung back the chair, yanked open the center drawer, and grabbed her mom's necklace... for her dad.

She rushed back to the storm cellar. The wind whipping her hair. Her heart pounding so loud in her ears, it drowned out the sirens.

Elisi pulled Wren inside and slid the heavy latch into place.

They backed away from the door, down the steps, and held on to each other as the angry wind snapped, crashed, and hurled things around them. And they held their breath and waited for the sound of a freight train—the sound of a tornado.

Instead, they heard the sirens die out like a super-loud set of leaky bagpipes.

Then eerie quiet.

They stayed put and listened to the weather radio to make sure there was no round two. Then Elisi nodded her belief it was safe. Together, they pushed opened the cellar door and prepared themselves to survey the damage.

The power was out, things were a mess, but they had been lucky. A tree by the driveway missed Elisi's truck by inches. Trash cans had been thrown against the house like a pair of dice. A Halloween skeleton, from who knows where, landed face down by the front door, as if a neighbor had decomposed on his way for a visit.

They had survived. They were safe. Wren checked her phone and thankfully had service. She scrolled through the alerts. Looked like the town of Wagoner, just to the northwest of them, was hit pretty hard.

Elisi whirled around, her eyes flashing. "What were you thinking? Leaving me like that. Don't you ever do that again. Do you understand me? I can't—" Her face went pale, and her knees buckled.

Wren rushed to catch her before she could fall and helped her sit on the front steps. Wren joined her. "I'm sorry, Elisi. I didn't mean to scare you." But as she slipped her hand in her pocket and her hand closed around her mom's necklace, she knew, without a doubt, she would do the same thing all over again.

Chapter Twenty-Eight

The muted hum of chain saws chewing through tree bark woke her. Wren pulled back the curtain and looked out the window at the bright blue cloudless sky. If she hadn't seen it with her own eyes, hadn't lived through it, she would've thought today was just another perfect October day instead of proof of Oklahoma weather doing another one-eighty.

Fort Gibson had been lucky. Technically, no tornado, only high winds. Still, it caused just enough damage to the school grounds that they had canceled classes for the day. But Wren's plans to sleep in were ruined by an overly productive neighborhood eager to get things cleaned up and back to normal.

Ever the non-morning person, she dragged herself toward the kitchen. The soles of her fuzzy slippers on the wood floor announced her impending arrival. She plodded over to Elisi and kissed her on the cheek. "Morning," she mumbled.

"Well, good morning, sunshine!" Elisi was back to her usual glee-filled self, scrambling eggs and frying hash browns for Elisi's Famous Potato, Egg & Cheese Breakfast Taquitos.

Wren's eyes lit up. A Whataburger PE&C Taquito and a large Dr Pepper with extra ice was, hands down, Wren's favorite breakfast, but unfortunately, the nearest Whataburger was about twenty miles away, so she didn't get it often. And now she was about to get the knock-off version without even asking. Surviving a near-death experience had its perks.

She grabbed a glass, chocked it to the brim with ice, and poured herself a Dr Pepper. She leaned back against the counter and took a long, syrupy, delicious sip. She sighed. No school on a school day and her favorite breakfast. Life was good.

"Your dad called," Elisi said over her shoulder. "He and some of the other officers are helping out over in Wagoner. He wanted to talk to you but didn't want to wake you. Said he'd be home as soon as he could."

Wren stopped mid-DP sip, remembering she still had her mom's necklace in her room. She sat her drink on the counter and snuck the necklace back in its rightful place. Her dad would be none the wiser.

She reclaimed her spot in the kitchen and watched, hungrily, as Elisi constructed Wren's dream taquito. So fat, it was hard to roll. They had skipped dinner with all yesterday's weather excitement, so Elisi knew Wren had to be starving.

The clammer of trash cans outside broke her taquito focus.

Elisi kept her attention on what she was doing. "He's been out there for hours. Waiting for somebody to get her lazy self out of bed. Best go tell him it's time for breakfast."

Wren's face scrunched in confusion. Then, realizing what Elisi was saying, her eyes widened as she looked down at herself. To her feet. To her pajamas. She could only imagine her hair. She slammed her glass down on the counter and ran to her room.

"If I can see you looking that way, why can't he?" Elisi yelled with a chuckle.

In five—okay, maybe ten—minutes flat, she had brushed

her teeth, washed her face, thrown on jeans and a sweatshirt, pulled her hair into a ponytail, slapped on a ballcap, and was back in the kitchen. It was a new world record.

Elisi looked up and nodded. "Impressive. Why can't you do that on a regular school day?"

Wren gave her a look that said, *Funny.*

Elisi waved her outside. "Breakfast is getting cold. Go get him."

Wren opened the front door to see Brantley, who had already picked up the broken branches, righted their trash cans, and was now raking the yard. He stopped and turned when he heard the door. He propped his hands on the rake and smiled. A big, glad-to-see-you-pearly-white smile made brighter by a face red from a mixture of work and cold.

Wren wrapped her arms around herself as the chilly air hit her. "What are you doing out here?"

He swept his hand across their almost back-to-pristine front yard. "Uh... isn't it obvious?" He pointed at the huge, uprooted tree by the driveway. "You guys are on your own with that."

Wren laughed and opened the door wider. "Elisi said breakfast is ready."

Brantley threw down the rake and headed for the door. "Now you're talking."

Elisi had come up behind Wren to hurry them inside. She took a look outside. "Brantley! Wado!" she said, thanking him for a job well done. "Now get yourself in here. I'm feeding you."

Wren scarfed her taquito down so fast she hardly had time to taste it. Brantley put away two to her one. When Wren's brain caught up and sent the signal she'd far surpassed the point of fullness, she sat back and groaned. "Ugh… That was so good, Elisi…. Wado… but ugh…"

Brantley nodded as he finished his last bite and swallowed. "Yes, ma'am. Thank you—I mean, wado."

Elisi chuckled. "You are still not ready for 'you're welcome' in Cherokee, so let me just say, you are welcome." She nodded at him. "And thank you again for all your hard work. Everything looks great." She sat down and wrapped her hands around her coffee mug to warm them. "So, any damage at your house?"

Brantley shook his head. "No ma'am."

Elisi waved him off. "Please, call me Elisi."

Wren chuckled. "You'd better. She means it."

"Okay, yes, ma'am—I mean, Elisi."

They all laughed

Elisi started clearing the table. "Now, shoo… I've got this. You two go. Get back to your investigating, or better yet, go out and enjoy this beautiful day the Creator saw fit to give to us."

They single-filed back to her room. Wren crashed across the bed. Brantley plopped into the Big Joe memory foam chair beside her. The one Wren had curled up in so many times with her mom for a bedtime story. The one that gave Wren her love of books.

"I gotta get me one of these," Brantley said, wallowing back and forth.

"Ugh… I ate too much," Wren moaned.

Brantley scoffed, "Yeah, right. Like that's a real thing."

They hung out in silence. Digesting. Wren, fairly certain she was never eating again.

Brantley looked like he wanted to say something but wasn't sure how to say it. He cleared his throat. "Hey, um… any word on that body they found—the one that's *not* your mom, I mean?"

Wren propped herself up on her elbow and shook her head. "Dad said it can take weeks for DNA. Dental records are quicker, but that won't work this time." She plopped back down flat and closed her eyes. "I was afraid to ask him what that meant."

The quiet returned for a while. Finally, Brantley slapped his hands down on the chair and changed the subject. "So... what's next? Should we pull out the murder board?"

Wren stayed flat on the bed, eyes closed, and said nothing.

She heard him slide the board out from under the bed and set it against the footboard. She sat up as he updated the board with the latest victim info they'd gotten from Landry. The location of the church was also inside the map's lopsided red circle.

"Nice going on getting all that out of Landry, by the way. Genuis actually. Surprised I didn't think of it myself."

He stared at the board, ignoring her comment, then shook his head. He dropped the marker. "This is getting us nowhere. This may work on TV, but it's not helping us solve anything." He stood up and flopped himself back down into the Big Joe. "We need another clue." He scoffed. "I mean, we need a *good* clue."

His words poked at her like they were systematically searching for something inside her brain. *Another clue... A good clue...* Wren bolted straight up the second she remembered and clambered off the bed. At her desk, she yanked open the center drawer and grabbed the card with Susan's security camera login and password. She held it up and smiled. "Fingers crossed. We might just have one."

Chapter Twenty-Nine

Wren motioned for Brantley to join her at her desk as she opened her laptop. "Susan—J.R.'s mom—gave me her login to her security cameras." She turned to look at Brantley, still rolling his way out of the foam chair. "I was just about to check the video out when my dad told me about them finding—anyway, I forgot all about it. Susan's house is right across from where Landry found the tortured cat." Her eyes danced with excitement. "Maybe the cameras caught something. Come on...let's see what we can see."

Brantley's face went pale and he fell right back into the chair. He held up a hand. "YOU see. And let me know."

Wren's excitement turned to a bit of a gut check. She didn't want to watch the poor thing being tortured either, but thankfully, in the few seconds of video she'd managed to see before her dad had called her into the living room, the area looked too far away from the camera to have really caught too much, if any, of the actual deed. *Hopefully*...She blew out a breath in relief, although she knew it wasn't very investigator-ly of her to think that way. A good detective would want the whole thing caught on video to help nail the sicko. But no need to tell Brantley about her hesitations. Best to have him think she was tougher than he was.

She twisted around to look at Brantley. "Okay, where should we start?"

Brantley tried to lean forward but the foam chair fought back. He laughed as he rolled out, walked over, and sat on the edge of the bed—closer, but not close enough to really see the screen. "Didn't you say you were there when Landry brought the cat in?"

"Yep. Couple Saturday's ago around two—three maybe?"

"If I was gonna look—and I'm not—I'd start there and go backward."

Wren nodded.

She was cautiously optimistic. Susan's area was mostly rural, and her cameras had night vision, so even from a distance, somebody parked or walking down the street should be easy to spot. That was something they could use.

She clicked on the day, dragged the progress bar on the video to a little past the time she thought Landry got back with the cat. She started scrolling backward looking for movement or any changes in the frame. Susan's cameras weren't set up for motion detection, so checking the whole thing was their only option.

Her hopes sank after going through and finding nothing. "Only UPS and the mailman Friday afternoon. And neither one of them stopped." She shrugged. "Should I go back farther?"

Brantley's brow furrowed. He checked the murder board, then spread the report copies across the bed until he found what he was looking for. "The cat was on the fence, right?"

"Yeah..."

His eyes scanned the report. He brought it over and laid it down on the desk beside her. He pointed to a box on the report form. "Here, it says the anonymous tip was at one-nineteen p.m. on Saturday, the same day we're looking at."

"But that doesn't mean that's when it happened."

He nodded. "Yeah, but if I've learned anything from watching reruns of *Law & Order*, I'm pretty sure it was the perp who called it in."

Wren's brow scrunched, not exactly following.

"You know . . . all proud-like—wanting somebody to see what they'd done." He sat back on the edge of the bed. "And even though there's not a lot of traffic around there, there's no way something like that hanging on a fence goes unnoticed. You said UPS and the mailman didn't stop. So…"

The light bulb went off. "Right!" Wren said. "The mailman went by first. We need to focus on the time between the UPS truck driving by on Friday and the tip being called in on Saturday." Wren turned back to the computer. "I must have missed something."

"And really, no way he would've done it in broad daylight, right? At least I don't think so." Brantley came over, put one hand on the desk and the other on the back of Wren's chair, and leaned over her shoulder. "I'd focus between the UPS truck and dawn."

"Got it." Wren, thankful for the extra set of eyes, decided against reminding him he hadn't wanted to watch.

Back to the video, she dragged the progress bar from just past first light all the way back to the UPS truck. This time even slower. Their eyes fixed on the screen, looking for even the tiniest movement.

Elisi's knock on the open bedroom door made them jump.

She laughed and held up a hand. "Looks serious. Sorry to interrupt. I'm just letting you know I'm headed to Tahlequah. Book club. Back in time for dinner." She made a circle with her finger toward the murder board and reports strewn across the bed. "And your dad called. He'll be home early."

Wren nodded. Message received.

Elisi kissed her fingers and threw the kiss into the room.

"What was that about?" Brantley asked after Elisi had left.

"Just my dad would freak if he caught us looking into this."

A nervous look came over Brantley's face. "Wha-what do you mean freak?"

Wren looked at him closely, remembering the bruised wrist, the busted lip. She wasn't sure what she should say, only that now was the time to say it. She ran her tongue over her teeth, searching for moisture. "Uh… look… I-I don't want to make you mad, or be all nosy or anything, but is everything okay with *your* dad?"

His jaw clenched. "What are you talking about?"

"The bruise on your wrist, the split lip. And your bike…not a scratch." She held up her hands. "Hey, I'm not saying there *is* anything wrong, but if there is, my dad can help.… I want to help."

He stiffened and, for an instant, his hands balled into fists as if preparing to fight. Wren braced herself. Not for a physical blow, but a mind-your-own-business-we're-no-longer-friends punch that would be a thousand times more painful.

But just as suddenly, he walked over and sat back down on the edge of the bed. He stared at the floor as if the words he was trying to find were hidden deep in the pattern of the rug. He blew out a long breath. His fingers uncurled. "It's… complicated," he said finally. "My dad... he gets angry sometimes. Once my mom bailed, that left me and my brother. Basically, he takes it out on whoever's closest." He looked up at her and shrugged in a no-big-deal way. "So, I try not to be around much." He smiled, as if that was a totally acceptable solution to such an unimaginable problem. "I'm okay. Really. No help needed. I can take care of myself."

Wren didn't say anything, only nodded, or thought she did. Honestly, she went kind of numb. She had asked. Had opened that door. Suspected even.

She chewed on her bottom lip. Now, what was she supposed to do with the information? Take him at his word that he was okay? That he could take care of himself? He had confided in her so quickly, it was like he'd been waiting for someone to ask.

He stood up, as if signaling time for a subject change. He pulled the stool she used to reach the top of her closet over to the desk and straddled it. "Let's just finish this."

"Oh... uh... one sec." Wren, remembering her dad would be coming home soon, jumped up, and in one swift movement, pulled the murder board out flat, piled the report copies on top, and slid the board under the bed. Not so much as a spec of evidence of their investigation remained.

She turned to Brantley's clearly impressed face and laughed. "Oh, trust me, I can do it even faster if necessary."

She came back to the desk, sat down, and turned the screen so they both could see. Backtracking obviously wasn't working, so this time, they were going to go forward and watch it in real time, starting Friday evening at dusk.

She hit play.

If it hadn't been for the occasional white blob of an insect darting in front of the camera, Wren would've doubted the video was running. Her body tensed. Watching nothing on an eerie green night vision screen with Brantley's admission echoing in her head was like watching a scary movie waiting for something to jump out at her.

"Wait—" He brought his face closer to the screen. "What was that? Go back."

She hit rewind, then play again.

"There," he said.

Wren hit pause to freeze the image, and moved closer to the screen.

It was the front end of an old truck with its light off, that had pulled into the left side of the camera frame and stopped. It was such a slight movement, it was no wonder she'd missed it earlier.

The truck stayed parked there for almost forty-five minutes. Plenty long enough to do something so horrible.

She watched, glued to the screen, looking for anything that might be a clue, until the truck backed away, as if somehow sensing the camera was watching.

Brantley straightened. "Play it again." His voice sounded strange.

She sighed. "What's the use? It's a crappy angle. We can't see the driver, the license tag—"

"Play it again."

She shook her head and set it up to replay.

"STOP."

She froze the video on the front end of the truck.

"Zoom in. Can you zoom in?"

It took Wren forever to figure out how, but she finally

managed to enlarge the small section of truck. She stood, almost knocking over her chair. She was over it. "This is stupid. *I'm* stupid for thinking we could solve this."

She flipped her hand toward the computer. "That's nothing. We'll never figure out who that is."

The muscles in Brantley's jaw tensed as he stared at the grainy image. "We don't have to figure out who it is," he said, his voice flat.

Wren scrunched her face. "What? Why?"

He pointed to the screen. "That truck... that's my brother's."

Chapter Thirty

Wren's jaw dropped. The shock of Brantley's words took her breath away. She reached back and fumbled to find her chair and fell into it. She did a quick shake of her head, as if that could remotely help her register what he'd just said. "Wha—what?" she stuttered. "What do you mean? How can you tell?" She peered at the frozen frame on the screen. "Are you sure?"

"There…" Brantley pointed. "See that dent right above the wheel? That was me. I did that. And boy, did I catch—yeah…," he scoffed. "I'm sure."

Wren stared at him, unsure what the proper reaction should be to finding out a family member liked to torture and kill animals. It wasn't as if Brantley had known it all along, but now that he did, he didn't seem all that surprised. Her heart and stomach cramped into one big, knotted ball. "Geez, Brantley" was all she could say. She hurt for him. His father… now his brother? She couldn't make her mouth close. What was it like, living in that house? How did he live with all that and still come out good? Come out *him*?

Brantley ran his hand down his face and met her eyes. "Now what?"

"Hey, I get he's your brother…," she said gently, "but we can't let him get away with this, right?"

Brantley sat there, staring toward the window, as if running what-ifs in his head.

Wren finally broke the silence. "I think we should tell Landry."

Brantley sighed and brought his eyes back to her. "Look, that's my brother's truck. I'm sure of it. But that's not really proof of anything." He paused. "It's just, my brother—he—he hasn't had it so easy." Brantley dipped his head and lowered his voice. "My dad's a lot harder on him."

The front door opened and shut. "I'm home," her dad's voice boomed. "I've got pizza!"

Wren bolted up out of the chair and headed for the door.

Brantley caught her by the arm. "Look, Wren, I don't want to make things harder for him without proof. Please…" His eyes begged her. "Don't say anything yet."

He had a point. The truck, by itself, wasn't enough. Maybe he let somebody borrow it. And now, knowing what went on in his house, she didn't want to make things worse for him or his brother on the chance they might be wrong. She nodded.

She headed for the dining room. Brantley followed.

Her dad plopped down two pizza boxes and a six-pack of Dr Pepper on the table, and took off his jacket. He walked over and held out his hand. "You must be Brantley. Pleasure to meet you."

"Nice to meet you too, sir."

Wren's dad raised his brow. "Manners. Nice to see. Most kids—"

"Daaaad…"

Her dad held up his hands in surrender. "Okay, okay. No more generational judging." He motioned to the table. "It's pizza night, Brantley. Elisi got held up in Tahlequah. She'll be home later. I told her I'd do dinner duty. Please, join us."

"That's okay, Mr. Mac—"

Her dad held up a hand again. "Nonsense. Elisi told me all about how hard you worked on our yard today. It looks great. Thank you. The least I can do is feed you. I insist." He opened the pizza boxes. The smell of melted cheese, stuffed crust, and warm cardboard hit them in the face. Wren decided she could eat again after all. Brantley's stomach growled.

Her dad handed them each a plate. "We have pepperoni and pepperoni. What's your pleasure?"

Wren could see hesitancy all over Brantley's face. They'd gotten so caught up in things, they hadn't eaten since breakfast. For somebody who was hungry twenty-four/seven, even if their discovery had ebbed his appetite, he still had to be starving.

She walked behind him and pulled out a chair for him, then went to the other side of the table.

His stomach got the best of him. He sat down and grinned. "Umm... pepperoni?"

"Excellent choice," her dad said as he scooted the box closer to Brantley. He pointed at Brantley's hat. "I see you're a Cubbies fan. Me too. They need all the support we can give them. But, unfortunately, no hats at the table. House rule."

Wren rolled her eyes and let out a deep sigh. After everything Brantley had already been through, plus what he'd just found out—now this? "Geez, Dad, way to make him welcome."

Brantley stopped her. "It's okay. No problem. Yes, sir." He winced as he slowly took off the Cubs hat that was covering a two-inch crusted-over gash. The cut was dark and red around the edges as if it was as irritated as Wren felt. Brantley quickly tried to cover it with his hair, but no way he was hiding *that*.

Her dad grimaced. "Ouch, that looks like it hurts. What happened there?"

Wren had a pretty good idea.

Brantley brought his hand up to cover it, not answering the question. He shifted uneasily in his chair and looked sheepishly at her father. "Sorry. Want me to put it back on?"

"No, no, no," her dad said, eyeing the wound. "Looks like it could do with a little air."

Brantley gave them both a nervous little grin, then deflected by going all in on the pizza.

Smart, Wren thought. As long as his mouth was full, he couldn't answer any questions.

Wren helped get him out of the hot seat by switching to the standard how-was-your-day-type stuff. Unfortunately, the conversation accidentally took a wrong turn toward Wren and Brantley's English project.

"Now, what's it supposed to be about?" her dad asked.

Wren straightened in her chair and used her best Mrs. Myers voice. "A shared legacy: how to work together to leave a mark."

Her dad cocked a brow. "Interesting... and how exactly are you two planning to leave this mark?"

Wren and Brantley looked at each other. Even at school, sitting in Mrs. Myers's class, the case had been the only thing on their minds. They hadn't even thought about the project, or at least a cover story.

She shrugged. "Well... umm..."

Her dad leaned back in his chair. "And it's due when?"

She waved him off. "Oh, it'll be okay. It's a ten-to-twenty-minute oral report. I can talk that much by myself."

Her dad held up a hand. "PREACH!" Then he shrugged. "What? Too old? Hey, I'm just trying to be cool, man."

Wren covered her face with her hands.

Brantley laughed. A very good sign given everything. Wren couldn't help but be amazed. And she thought *she* was resilient.

When they were finished, Wren stood and started clearing the table. Brantley followed her lead.

Her dad stopped them. "I've got this. You guys get back to your project. And, Brantley, if I were you, I'd figure out how you're going to get a word in edgewise."

Brantley chuckled. Wren playfully punched his arm.

"Thanks for the pizza, Chief MacIntosh."

Her dad nodded. "You're welcome. Thank you for all your help on the yard. And please, call me Chief."

Back in her room, Wren pushed the door halfway closed behind them, knowing her dad wouldn't like it closed all the way—another house rule. But it had been so long since she'd had a friend over, it was never an issue.

Brantley plopped down in the Big Joe. His face fell, as if the temporary reprieve the pizza and laughter provided had suddenly worn off.

If his crushed expression hadn't been enough to tug at her heart, there was that horrible, ugly cut on his forehead. "Be right back," she said.

She went to Elisi's bathroom, opened the medicine cabinet, and sifted through the shelf of Cherokee remedies until she found the one she was looking for. A small glass jar with CUTS scribbled across the black lid in silver Sharpie. Elisi, being her thoughtful self, had labeled the various bottles and jars in English for Wren and her dad in case she wasn't home. Although her dad preferred to use the mass-marketed chemical versions from the corner drug store.

Elisi would always shake her head when one of the many drug commercials came on the screen—especially when the possible side effects sounded worse than what you were taking them for. "Such a waste of money when you can get what you need from nature," she would lean over and whisper to Wren. "No need for a middleman."

Wren hurried back to her room and handed Brantley the whole jar, knowing Elisi wouldn't mind. "Here…"

Brantley took the jar, opened the lid, and stuck it under his nose. He scrunched his face.

Wren rolled her eyes. "Seriously? It's not that bad. Besides, I didn't say eat it." She motioned toward his head. "Put it on your cut. A couple times a day. Trust me, it'll help. And no hats." It struck her how much she sounded like Elisi.

Brantley's look said he was skeptical.

Wren stuck her face right in front of him. She pointed to her chin. "See this scar right here?"

He leaned forward and squinted his eyes. "Nope."

She straightened and put her hands on her hips. "Exactly."

He held up his hands. "Okay, okay." He slipped the jar in his jacket pocket. "Thanks."

"You're welcome." She sat down on the edge of the bed across from him, not knowing what to say. Helping with the cut on his head had been easy. But she could tell by his face, by the way he sat crumpled in the chair, he was hurt on the inside, too. If only

Elisi's cabinet held a bottle that could keep those kinds of hurts from leaving a scar.

Her dad knocked on the door and pushed it all the way open. "The station just called. Another suspected arson out on the edge of town. I've got to go."

Wren's mind went straight to the poor animals from the barn fire. It must have shown on her face.

"Far as I know, it's just an old shed. No loss of life. However, Elisi may still be a while, and I don't know how long I'll be. A few minutes is one thing, but I'm afraid I'm old-school. I'm sorry, son, but I'm going to have to ask you to leave. Can I drop you off?"

Brantley scrambled out of the chair. "No, it's okay," he said, zipping his jacket and gathering his things. "I need to get home anyway to—" He cut his eyes to Wren. "Uh—stuff. I've got my bike."

The three of them walked to the front door, her dad leading the way.

"Thanks again for the pizza," Brantley said as he picked up his bike.

Her dad waved and gave Brantley a quick smile as he got into his car.

Brantley quickly turned back toward Wren. "'K. See you in class. We'll come up with a plan." He leaned in even though there was no way her dad could hear. "Thanks for not saying anything."

Her nod said, *Okay*, but as Wren went back inside, closed the door, and leaned up against it, she was pretty sure she already had a plan.

And she was definitely sure Brantley wasn't going to like it.

Chapter Thirty-One

Mrs. Myers surprised everyone with a free period. "Presentations are due next week, so I want to give each team some extra time. We'll get through as many as we can starting Monday and continue until everyone's had their chance." She pulled off her glasses and used them to point at the class. "Fair warning. I'll be drawing names again to determine the team order, so everyone should be prepared to present on Monday, just in case."

Wren groaned as everyone shuffled seats to get next to their partners. She had absolutely no interest in doing this project—or sitting through nine others. What she and Brantley were trying to do was a real-life make a difference—not make-believe-for-a-grade wishes.

Although, she had to admit, ridding Fort Gibson of an animal killer would be perfect for their presentation and surely get them a passing grade. But then, Brantley would have to stand in front of the class and tell them his brother's a psycho.

After their discovery, she halfway expected Brantley to skip school. Not that she had one, but if it were her brother, she'd curl up in bed, pull the covers over her head, and stay there.

But in English class he was. And not even late.

He got up from his desk, walked to the back of the room, and sat down beside her.

She felt bad for him, but what could she say? What could possibly make him feel any better? "Elisi said for you to come to dinner."

It was all she could think of.

She reached down into her backpack, pulled out her laptop, and opened it. A wallpaper-sized photo of her mom smiled back at her. A wave of guilt washed over her. She hadn't checked her missing websites, alerts, or even thought about snooping around her dad's office for clues in days. It was a gut punch to realize that, just for a moment, she had forgotten. And in doing so, had let her mother down.

Hot tears pooled in the corners of her eyes.

She looked away from the laptop, unable to look at her mother's face, her smile.

"Hey, you okay?" Brantley's face was filled with concern.

She raised a finger for him to give her a minute while she tried to mentally talk herself down. She wasn't the only one looking for her mom, she knew that now. And what if they'd already found her? She didn't believe the remains were her mother, but she couldn't honestly say if her gut feeling was genuine intuition or just wishful thinking. She knew herself well enough to know she would land on the side of hope every time.

She felt a sudden warmth spread over her. Envelop her. Calm her. As if, in some mystical way, she'd been taken into her mother's arms. As if her mom's spirit, from wherever it was, had traveled across the miles to tell her, *No guilt. No regrets. Only love.*

Wren crossed her hands on her chest and closed her eyes. Her tears pooled and fell down her face. When she finally opened her eyes she saw Brantley, still staring at her, looking ready to bolt to get Mrs. Myers.

"I—I'm okay...," she said as she dabbed at her face with the sleeves of her sweatshirt.

Brantley shot out of his chair and up to Mrs. Myers's desk—the front corner of which had been occupied for some time with enough tissues and hand sanitizer to disinfect a middle-grade army. Mrs. Myers looked up and smiled as he pulled a handful of tissues from the box.

But what Wren wanted more than tissues was a way to slow time. A way to cling to this feeling—this closeness with her mother just a little longer before it faded away

And it did. Fade away. But instead of being sad because it had left her, she felt only gratitude it had come.

"Thanks." Wren took the tissues from Brantley and made a cursory swipe of her nose, but she had already regrouped and was back to normal. Her normal, anyway. She could tell he was curious. Wanted to know what had happened. But that would stay between Wren and her mom.

She motioned for him to scoot his chair closer. She leaned in, lowered her voice, and in a direct, no-nonsense way that sounded just like her cop father, ripped off the proverbial Band-Aid. "I've got to tell Landry about your brother."

The look on his face made her regret her delivery, but not the message.

She softened her tone. "I'm sorry, that didn't come out right. But look, you can't ask your brother and you can't talk to Landry. You're not even supposed to know anything about it.

This all happened because I stole the reports, remember?" She grimaced. "Landry's not gonna be happy about that."

She gave Brantley a reassuring smile. "But it'll be okay. You'll see. Landry's cool. He'll ask your brother what his truck was doing around there when it happened." She shrugged. "Maybe he's got an excuse. Maybe if it wasn't him, he saw something or whatever. Landry's not gonna go blabbing about it to anybody. That's against the rules. Besides, he's not like that. I trust him."

Brantley stayed silent.

Wren got it. He was torn between giving his brother a heads-up and upsetting his father or letting them both be blindsided.

She touched his arm. "Trust me. It will be better if you stay out of it."

He slowly nodded, but she couldn't tell if he agreed.

They sat in silence for the remainder of the class—mostly. With an occasional point at the laptop screen to make it look like they were working. In reality, Wren was running all the worst-case scenarios through her mind. And there were plenty.

"Okay, class," Mrs. Myers interrupted. "Time's almost up. Let's get our desks back where they belong before the bell rings."

Myers might as well have said, "Ready ... set ... go." The classroom erupted in a cacophony of scoots, scrapes, and squeals across the badly-in-need-of-wax floor, that hurt Wren's teeth like fingernails on chalkboard.

Brantley got up to move. Wren reached out to stop him. She looked around to make sure nobody was close enough to hear. "I'll go see Landry right after school. I'll text you after. Then come over for dinner, okay?"

Brantley nodded, still looking stunned. For the first time

ever, the mention of Elisi's cooking couldn't coax even a hint of a smile. Was he mad at her? In shock? She couldn't tell. But doing the right thing here was bigger than both of them.

The bell rang. The mass exodus ensued. Wren and Brantley headed toward the door.

"Happy Halloween," Mrs. Myers yelled over the commotion. "Make good choices."

Halloween? Wren had been riding past jack-o'-lanterns, ghost, and skeletons for weeks now. She had been so wrapped up with this case, the fact that tonight was Halloween had totally escaped her. She caught up to Brantley. "I ... mean ... come over, if you don't already have plans." Wren only had plans if handing out candy with Elisi counted.

Finally, Brantley gave her a sly grin. "I'm going to M.J.'s party. Aren't you?"

They both laughed. M.J.'s Halloween parties were supposedly epic. A middle-grader showing up would never live to walk the halls of Fort Gibson High.

"What about your brother? Is he going?"

Brantley laughed so loud, he snorted. "Uh ... they don't exactly run in the same circles."

Wren had forgotten what M.J. had said at McDonald's. Guess the guest list wouldn't include somebody you'd called a freakazoid stalker—unless it was their costume.

She definitely wasn't looking forward to the conversation with Landry and what it could mean—banned from the shelter—telling her dad, but she also wanted to get it over with. Get the weight of it off her before another animal is hurt or worse, whatever the consequences.

She hurried toward her locker. Brantley followed close behind, as if maybe trying to think of a way to make her reconsider. But her mind was made up.

Their teachers had granted mercy from homework for Halloween, so Wren's plan was to dump everything from her backpack except her laptop. As she got to her locker, she stopped. Sticking out of the locker vents were feathers.

Three guesses where they came from.

Brantley's jaw dropped.

M.J. didn't do it herself. That was certain. Coming inside, getting the stench of middle school on her, was beneath her. No, she'd sent one or both of her minions. Ever since Wren had gone off on her, M.J. had given her a wide berth, but apparently, she couldn't resist the urge to be a bully-by-proxy.

Brantley shook his head, disgusted. "What a grade-A b—"

"This doesn't bother me," Wren interrupted. She pulled the feathers from the vent and looked them over. "She's not even smart enough to know she actually gave me a gift."

She waved it off. "But I can't deal with this right now." She opened her locker and placed the feathers carefully on the shelf, then smiled at Brantley. "I'll take them home later and Elisi can tell us what kind they are."

Wren slammed the locker shut and they headed toward the bike racks. Wren stopped. Her stomach knotted with a sudden thought. "Tonight is Halloween.... Halloween and animals—not a good mix. Look, I'm not saying it is your brother, but if it is, he might be planning something."

Brantley looked sick.

"Listen, I'll go talk to Landry. But you... you've got to keep an eye on your brother."

Chapter Thirty-Two

She should've known Landry wouldn't be at the shelter on Halloween. He'd be patrolling the streets, eyes peeled for anyone looking to cause trouble.

She sat on her bike in front of the shelter and considered her next move. Her suspicions—let alone her confessions, weren't something she could tell him by phone. *"Hey Landry, I dug through your office, stole some reports from your desk, I think it's one killer, and I know who it is."* And it definitely wasn't a text. No, this was a face-to-face.

For Brantley's sake, she would try to make it sound like she believed it might not be his brother. But her gut, her finder feelings, her intuition, Holy Spirit, or whatever, told her, without a doubt, 100 percent, he was the one.

She couldn't ask Landry to come back to the shelter to look at the video. He probably wouldn't anyway. Besides, the horror of that night had already happened. If pulling him from patrol made him miss something he could've prevented, it would haunt her forever.

She chewed the inside of her cheek and toyed with the idea of telling her dad instead. No. She shook her head. Even if she copped to stealing the reports, Landry might get in trouble for not securing his office. Definitely no more shelter for her. And no more unchaperoned time in her dad's office, either, once he found out he could no longer trust her. When this was over, she needed to get back to searching for her mom, and she couldn't afford to lose that privilege.

She sighed, now knowing what people mean with they say something's a no-win situation.

No, all she could do for now was to go home and trust that Brantley could keep an eye on his brother.

She zipped up her too-light jacket and rubbed her hands together like she was trying to start a fire. She shivered. Her nerves may have kept her warm on the ride over, but now that she had to wait until tomorrow to talk to Landry, the chilly air cut right through her. A preoccupied mind and a quick change in the weather had definitely caught her unprepared.

As she wound her way down the side streets, she passed the rows of houses primed for the onslaught of trick-or-treaters. The hustle and bustle of costumes and candy wouldn't start until dusk, so for now, it was almost deserted.

The brisk ride bit at her face and her hands, but she had a system. Stuff one hand in her jacket pocket, just long enough to thaw, then switch. She pulled the neck of her jacket up over her chin but most of her face was on its own.

Everything around her screamed Halloween. She took in a frosty breath. Was it weird Halloween had a smell? The moon, when it rose, would add its own touch of spooky, turning the silhouettes of the naked trees into towering, hungry-for-souls goblins.

The prospect of such a perfectly eerie Halloween made Wren pedal faster. Even with everything going on, knowing there was nothing she could do tonight to fix things, she still looked forward to spending the evening with Elisi—and now Brantley. Handing out candy, oohing and aahing over the costumes, watching scary movies in between rings of the doorbell. It had become another one of their traditions. The thought made her smile as another crossed her mind. How nice it would be if her dad could join them.

But that was more than she could hope for with all the craziness that comes with Halloween.

She slammed on the brakes. Her back wheel locked and skidded to a stop. She stood, straddling her bike with her mouth open, not wanting to believe what she was seeing.

Across a vacant field, on the next road over, not far from where she'd found J.R., was Brantley's brother. She'd only seen him from a distance, in the parking lot at school, but her finder feelings told her it was him.

And it was definitely him tying a full-grown German shepherd into the back of his truck.

The truck.

She coasted her bike behind an overgrown shrub so she wouldn't be out in the open. She sucked in her breath and dug her phone out of her pocket as fast as her almost-numb fingers would allow and hit Landry's number.

Voicemail. Again. She grimaced through his too-long message, waiting for the beep.

"It's me, Wren," she said breathless, cupping her hand over her mouth like there was some crazy chance her words would float all the way across the field, and he might hear her. "Listen, I'll explain later, but I think I know who hurt that cat—maybe all the animals."

The slam of the truck's tailgate took her attention away from the phone. Brantley's brother stopped to pet the shepherd before climbing into the driver's side. Him, showing the dog kindness, making the poor thing trust him, when God only knew what he had in mind, turned Wren's stomach.

It also made her miss leaving Landry the rest of her message.

She quickly called back, hoping if Landry saw it was her again, he'd figure it was important.

The truck engine roared, but he didn't move. Wren prayed it was because he had a change of heart.

Her brain went into overdrive. She glanced around. There was nobody around who could help her. For a second, she thought about yelling at him, *Hey! That's my dog!* or something. But she'd have to get a lot closer, and if she rode up next to the truck, what if instead of letting the dog go, he grabbed her, too? She had no idea what he was capable of. Judging by what he had done to that cat, she didn't want to find out the hard way.

Maybe it wasn't her smartest thought, and she was sure the German shepherd would agree, but she wanted Landry to catch him in the act. Of course, before the shepherd was hurt, but for there not to be any doubt.

She kicked the top pedal into position, getting into ready-to-go mode, as she waited for the stupid voicemail beep again. "Come on," she muttered, her eyes locked on the truck.

"Leave a message after the beep."

The truck started to move.

"Landry, it's me again…" Her voice was now frantic. "He's got a dog in his truck. I think he's going to hurt it. I'm going to try to follow him. Call me."

She shoved her phone in her pocket and took off.

He drove slowly and stayed on the side roads, which made it easier. She couldn't keep up, but all the stop signs helped her keep his taillights within sight. She had a horrific thought. What if he was cruising around looking for another fence to tape the dog to? What would she do then?

Wren watched in horror as he hit the gas and, just like that, he was gone.

She pulled up to the intersection and fought to catch her breath. Tears fell from her face. She rubbed the center of her chest with the heel of her hand to loosen the tightness. How could she have been so foolish, thinking she could follow a truck on a bike? Why hadn't she tried to stop him when she had the chance? She'd been selfish. She could've saved the shepherd and dealt with the fallout later. At least the shepherd...

Her only option was to call her dad now, pray to God he believed her, and hope he could find Brantley's brother before it was too late.

But her heart sank, knowing how that would go. Her finder feelings and the promise of a snippet of a video frame on her laptop wouldn't be enough proof for her by-the-book father. Not in time, anyway. Besides, even if he did agree to send out a car, where would he send it?

She couldn't just stay here. Do nothing.

An idea hit her. She could call dispatch—have Shelly patch her through to Landry's radio. Maybe then she could reach him. Maybe he'd believe her and know what to do.

She dragged her sleeve under her nose, and went for her phone, but before she could hit the police department's number, it rang.

It was Brantley.

She swiped to accept. She started to tell him what she had seen, but he didn't give her the chance.

"My brother just came home and drove straight back behind the garage," he practically shouted into the phone. "Oh my God, Wren. He's got a big dog in the back of the truck—I saw it."

Wren's heart leaped. It wasn't too late. They could still stop him. They could still save the shepherd. She was so happy, she had to fight to keep from busting into incoherent sobs. "I—I'll call Landry. I'm close. I'll be right there." She tightened her grip on her phone. "Brantley, don't let him hurt that dog."

"Got it. Hurry!"

Her phone dinged—an incoming call notification. She pulled it away from her ear to check. "It's Landry," she said, breathless. "Brantley, be careful!"

She clicked over to Landry and quickly filled him in. Not once did he sound like he thought she was crazy. He. Just. Believed. Her. She wanted to cry again.

"Garage... Sims' Residence...," Landry repeated. "I'll get the address from dispatch and be right out. And, Wren, promise me you won't go in until I get there."

Knowing full well there was no way she would ever keep it, once again, she said the two words no good P.I.—detective—cop—let alone a twelve-year-old amateur finder, should ever say: "I promise."

Chapter Thirty-Three

It took less than ten minutes for her to get to Brantley's house, but it seemed like forever. She stopped at the curb and nervously looked around. No vehicles in the driveway—Brantley's dad must not be home.

And no sign of Landry's truck.

She called Brantley. No answer.

Loud, piercing barks coming from behind the house made her heart race.

And then she remembered. She was Wolf Clan. A protector.

She ditched her bike at the edge of the driveway and ran toward the garage. The side door was ajar. Her heart thumped against the walls of her chest as if begging her feet to stop, but she didn't listen—couldn't listen.

She sucked in her breath. "Please, help me," she prayed as her trembling hand reached for the door.

She slipped inside as quietly as possible and pressed herself against the wall. Think. The goal—save the shepherd. The plan—not exactly clear.

She squinted her eyes, trying to force them to adjust. The only light, a dirty, yellowish glow, was coming from the back of the garage in what looked like some kind of workroom.

The barks grew louder. Pure straight-line adrenaline pounded in her ears as she inched closer.

"SHUT UP!" An angry voice. A loud thud. A sickening whimper.

She gasped and covered her mouth. She no longer cared that she didn't have a plan. She only knew she wasn't about to hear that sound again. She rushed toward the amber light, not seeing the dark heap on the floor. It sent her sprawling, knocking over paint cans, scrap wood, gardening tools, and whatever else could make the maximum amount of noise.

She scrambled to her feet, whirled around, and raised her hands in defense.

Brantley's brother spun around; his eyes grew wide. "WHAT TH—" He was standing with a roll of duct tape in his hand. The shepherd, chained to the leg of the worktable, was doing his best to stay away from him.

Wren's eyes went to the pile she'd tripped over. Her heart sank.

"Brantley!" She rushed to him, fell to her knees, and cradled his head. He was still breathing, thank God, but when she pulled back, blood covered her hands. She turned to Brantley's brother and glared at him, her anger searing away her fear. "What did you do?" she screamed. "What's wrong with you?"

He motioned toward the unconscious Brantley. "That's his own fault. You get in my business, there's bound to be consequences." He nodded. "Now he knows." He tilted his head and looked at Wren, a smile slowly forming on his face. "Are you going to get in my business?"

Suddenly, the shepherd darted from under the table and lunged for him. The chain clanked and strained against the workbench leg, biting into the dog's neck.

Startled, Brantley's brother fell back and scrambled out of range of the huge, snarling head of angry bared teeth.

It was just enough of a distraction. Wren grabbed a shovel from off the floor, brought it up, and swung as hard as she could.

She missed, hitting the edge of table instead. He charged. She swung again.

The metallic clunk of a heavy metal shovel against the side of a human head makes a sickening sound. Brantley's brother stood for a moment, his eyes wide, as if unsure what had happened.

Wren raised the shovel again, ready to strike another blow, when blood gushed from his now matted hair and snaked down his neck, staining his shirt in wide splotches of crimson. He touched the wetness with his fingertips, stared at his red hand, and gave her a strange, quizzical look, as if honestly asking her, *Why?*

He collapsed onto the floor.

Wren dropped to her knees, keeping a tight hold on the shovel. In every scary movie she'd ever seen, the victim drops the weapon beside the presumed-dead killer. Every. Time. And every time, she and her dad would yell, in unison, "STUPID!"

Rule number one: The killer's not really dead.

Rule number two: For Pete's sake, don't leave a weapon right beside them they can pick up and kill you with.

She stared at Brantley's brother and finally, his chest rose. She blew out a breath, relieved she hadn't actually killed him. He looked pretty unconscious though—and looked like he'd be that way for a while, but her grip stayed tight on the handle of the shovel anyway.

Brantley moaned.

Wren spun around and ran to him, dropping the shovel by his side, instead.

He sat up and winced as he rubbed his head. When his eyes finally focused, he saw his bleeding brother sprawled out on the floor. He scrambled over to him. "What—"

"I'm sorry!" Wren cried. "I had to!"

Brantley stumbled to the table and grabbed a roll of paper towels. He pressed it against the oozing gash on his brother's head. He looked up at Wren, his eyes pleading. "We gotta get him help."

Wren reached into her back pocket. It was empty. "My phone!" She scanned the workroom floor. "It must've..." She looked back at Brantley.

Brantley shook his head. "He smashed mine when I tried to stop him." Taking one hand away from the bloody paper towels, he felt in his brother's pockets and shook his head again. "Maybe his phone's in the truck. Go! Get help! Hurry!"

After a quick glance to check on the shepherd, now calm and curled up in the corner, Wren sprinted toward the side garage door. Rushing outside, she was instantly blinded by the setting sun. She brought her hand up to shield her eyes.

"WREN! ARE YOU OKAY?"

The unmistakable voice of her dad. It was the absolute best thing she'd ever heard.

When she dropped her hand, she saw her dad, Landry, and two uniformed officers standing in front of her. Their vehicles, with their flashing red and blue lights, crisscrossed the driveway and front yard, forming a barricade.

"DAD!" She ran to him, crying.

He grabbed her shoulders and stepped back so he could get a look at her. "Are you hurt? What's going on here?"

She broke down and just shook her head. She pointed back at the garage. "Brantley...brother...ambulance...," she cried.

Her dad nodded, then gestured Landry and the other officers to the garage.

Landry brought his radio up. "Requesting medical at this location," then followed the other officers in.

Wren's swollen eyes looked up at her father. "I'm sorry, Dad.... I-I had to—oh my God, Dad, what if he dies? What if I killed him?" She buried her head in her hands. "I just wanted to stop him. I had to stop him."

Her dad pulled Wren closer and held her tight. "It'll be okay," he said, not as the by-the-book chief of police, but in the soft, reassuring voice of her father. "Whatever happens, Wrenie, we'll deal with it. I've got you."

Wren melted into him, finally feeling safe.

Officer Dooley poked his head out the side garage door. "Chief, you'd better come take a look at this."

Her dad nodded and gave Wren a little squeeze. "You stay here with Landry."

Landry, who had just stepped back outside, had replaced the poor shepherd's chain for a much more comfortable leash and was walking to the truck with him.

Wren went over and leaned against the open tailgate. Landry handed her the leash. She bent down and stroked the shepherd's beautiful black-and-tan coat as he plopped down on the grass at her feet. Landry went to the truck and brought the dog some water.

As they stood side-by-side, Wren nudged Landry with her shoulder. "Thanks for coming."

He nudged her back. "I knew you wouldn't stay put until I got here, so I figured I'd better call in the cavalry."

Wren grinned and gave him a sheepish shrug. "Well… I couldn't help it."

He laughed. "Exactly."

She bit on her lip. "How bad did I hurt him?"

Landry put his arm around her. "You did a number on him, but he's still breathing." He leaned back and looked at her. "Brantley's brother, huh?" He let out a whistle. "Man, that sucks."

She nodded.

They stayed there for a while, not saying much, waiting for her dad. She sat down on the grass next to the shepherd to love on him and promptly got a huge head plopped in her lap. Today had been beyond stressful, but this… this dog, right here, right now, was all she needed.

She sighed, knowing what she had to do. Landry knew about J.R., had told Wren about the cat, and Susan's video was the clue that brought them here, but Wren needed to come clean and tell him the rest of it. She lowered her head. "I'm sorry, Landry. I went into your office when you weren't there and took pictures of all the abuse reports, trying to figure this whole thing out. Brantley's been helping me. We were just going to see if we could find something to bring to you. Really. But…" She motioned toward the garage. "It didn't really work out that way."

Landry was quiet as if needing time to consider what she'd just said.

She was afraid to look up at him, afraid she'd see anger, or worse, disappointment in his eyes.

Finally, he spoke. "Well… the report thing wasn't cool, but I think you already know that. I appreciate what you were trying to do, I only wish you would've trusted me with what you were doing. Wren, if this had gone badly, and something had happened to you, can you imagine how I would feel? How your dad and Elisi would feel?

Her head dropped lower. "I'm sorry."

Landry squatted down beside her and ran his hand down the shepherd and patted his hind quarters. "But I bet this friendly guy here is sure glad you cared enough to do something." He chuckled. "And that you didn't listen to me about staying outside." He paused. "Soooo… I guess that means so am I."

She looked at him, at his beautiful smile, when his face went suddenly serious. "But don't tell your dad I said that."

Relieved, she raised a finger. "Oh, one more thing… the whiteboard wasn't for school, it was our murder board."

He reared back with laughter. "Kiddo, you definitely have some cop in you."

She hunched over and gave the shepherd a head hug. He raised up and repaid her with a swipe up her face with the world's longest tongue. She scrunched up her face and laughed.

Landry laughed too. "That's *thank you for saving me* in German." He cocked a sly grin. "See what I did there? German… shepherd. Get it?"

Wren rolled her eyes. "You know, it's not as funny if you have to explain it."

Still, she chuckled as she wiped the dog slobbers away with her sleeve—discreetly so as not to hurt the dog's feelings—then kissed his long fuzzy muzzle, returning the favor. "You saved me, too, didn't you, big guy...," she said, peering into those big, beautiful, golden-brown eyes. "That makes us even."

The shepherd jumped up and started to howl, mimicking the wail of the ambulance approaching from down the street. Officer Owens hopped into his patrol car and moved it out of the way, allowing the ambulance to pull closer.

Doors flew open, bags were grabbed, a stretcher pulled from the back, in a single, fluid, well-practiced maneuver that sent two stone-faced EMTs hurrying toward the garage.

Seconds later, no doubt shooed away by the all-business EMTs, a dazed Brantley walked out of the garage, wrapped in a blanket someone had thrown over his shoulders, holding an ice pack to his head.

Wren rushed toward him, but stopped short as the front of the blanket came open. She gasped. His shirt and jeans were so soaked with his brother's blood that they clung to his skin. His hands clamped onto the edges of the blanket like a lifeline. Wren's stomach turned sour with guilt. She was only defending herself. She knew that. But she didn't mean to hurt Brantley's brother so badly.

It was just them. Brantley and Wren. Standing there. Her dad, the other officers, the EMTs were all still inside the garage. Landry was walking the shepherd around the property, letting him sniff things.

She fidgeted with the bottom edge of her jacket, while Brantley stood there, obviously in shock. She wanted to say something—anything helpful. But what could she say? *Sorry I almost killed your brother?*

The thundering rev of an engine made them look up. A

well-worn work truck barreled into the driveway, hurling gravel at anything unlucky enough to be close. The driver's-side door flung open before the truck came to a complete stop. A long, tall man who looked just like Brantley headed straight toward them, eyes angry and full of fire. "WHAT THE—"

"DAD!" Brantley's face drained of color, his whole body tensed.

Mr. Sims kept coming. "WHAT THE HELL DID YOU DO THIS TIME?" he growled.

The blanket dropped to the ground as Brantley's hands instinctively went up in defense. "I—I didn't—I promise."

Wren saw Brantley's dad curl his hand into a fist.

Without thinking, Wren stepped in front of Brantley as if, by some miracle, the laws of physics would cease to exist, and her twelve-year old body would somehow protect him. She braced herself for the blow.

Then. Nothing.

She opened her eyes. Wider.

Wren's dad had stopped Brantley's jerk-of-a dad's swing in midair.

She stepped back, pulling Brantley to safety with her.

Her dad's knuckles grew white as his grip tightened on Mr. Sims's wrist. The two men stood there, frozen, staring each other down.

Wren's dad narrowed his eyes. "Something tells me this isn't the first time you've raised a hand to your boys."

"MIND YOUR OWN DAMN BUSINESS," Sims snarled as he struggled to free himself.

Wren's dad swung the man's arm around and pinned it behind his back. "Officially, child abuse IS my business." He stepped closer to Mr. Sims's ear and lowered his voice. "Unofficially, if I see one more mark on that boy... today... tomorrow... next year... I promise, I'll come back here. And we can see how you do against somebody your own size."

He turned Mr. Sims loose and patted him on the shoulder in a now-that-we've-got-that-settled-let's-be-friends kind of way, just as the EMTs came out of the garage. Brantley's still-unconscious brother was strapped to the stretcher, an IV bag lying across chest. His head was wrapped in a coil of white gauze bandages.

Wren's breath caught, shocked at how much damage she'd done with one frantic swing of a shovel. She wanted to go to him—check on him—apologize to him, but her dad held her back and shook his head. Brantley's brother had done some horrible things and made it where she had no choice but to protect herself, but still, it made her heart hurt.

She looked over at Brantley as he watched them slide the stretcher into the ambulance. The pain in his face made her hurt for him, too.

She picked the fallen blanket off the ground and draped it across Brantley's shoulders, leaving her arm around him as if to say, *I'm so sorry. I'm here for you.* It was all she could think to do.

She closed her eyes to block the final image of the bottom of his brother's shoes before the ambulance doors slammed shut. And to thank God, Brantley was nothing like him.

Chapter Thirty-Four

"USDI!" Elisi cried, her face full of worry, her arms open wide.

Wren looked up, shocked to see her grandmother standing in front of the growing crowd that had gathered outside the stretch of yellow crime tape surrounding Brantley's house.

It was an odd feeling having ghosts, zombies, pirates, and princesses stare at you in the dark through the eerie effect of strobing police lights. A wall of parents and nosy neighbors behind them held phones in the air to commemorate the day's events for Facebook and YouTube. Happy Halloween.

Wren was almost to Elisi, but Officer Dooley beat her to it, raising the yellow crime scene tape allowing her to enter.

"Thank you, Dooley," Elisi said. She threw her arms around Wren and squeezed tight, then whispered in Wren's ear, "Thank God you're all right."

Dooley gestured as if tipping his hat. "Ma'am." He extended his arm out to guide them in the right direction.

Elisi looked back at the crowd. "Looks like you got your hands full."

Dooley nodded. "Yes, ma'am. You know what they say about small towns... news travels fast. Not sure why we bother using radios."

Elisi and Wren walked up the long driveway toward Brantley, stopping once so Elisi could catch her breath. "Good heavens. Now I know why they call them driveways instead of walkways." She chuckled, waving off Wren's look of concern. "I had to park back at the church. I'm fine. I've just exceeded my daily step allowance."

Landry pulled up next to them in his truck and rolled down his window. The shepherd, sitting up front, flew across the seat in search of some attention. Wren laughed and happily complied.

"I need to get this guy out of here," Landry said, pressed to the back of his seat trying to dodge a seriously wagging tail. "Doc Foley said he'd meet me back at his office and check him out. Plus, I bet he's hungry—that makes two of us."

Wren gave the dog one more scratch between the ears. "You are such a good boy," she said, leaning in for more kisses. "I'll see you at the shelter soon. I promise. You're in good hands."

Landry gently swept his arm against the shepherd's chest to guide the excited one-hundred-pound lapdog back to his rightful seat.

Landry gave Wren a smile. The good kind where the creases around his eyes got deep. "I'm really proud of you, kiddo. You did good."

Wren stepped back next to Elisi. "Thanks," she said, again, wiping the dog kisses away with her sleeve. Now that it was pretty much over, and she hadn't actually killed anybody, *and* the dog was still alive, a hint of a smile crossed her lips. She was kind of proud of herself too.

As Landry pulled away, he stuck his hand out the window. "But don't tell your dad I said that."

Wren chuckled, then wrapped herself around Elisi's arm.

Elisi patted Wren's hand and gave it a squeeze as they walked the rest of the way up to the garage. She chuckled. "Don't tell your dad... I'm proud of you, too."

They came upon Brantley, now sitting in the back of Dooley's running patrol car, his head against the window, eyes closed. Wren went to check on him, but Dooley held up his hand to stop her. "He was shivering. Thought I'd let him warm him up a little before—"

Wren's dad hurried up to them. "Elisi. Good. You're here." He gave Wren a quick hug. "You doing okay, sweetheart?"

Wren nodded.

His face tightened, his jaw shifted, as if deciding how much he should tell her. "Wrenie...this is much bigger than we initially thought."

Wren's eyes widened. "OH MY GOD! DID HE DIE? DID I KILL HIM?"

He put his hand on her shoulder. "No. No. No. He's going to be fine. Physically at least."

He ran his hand down his face, bending so they were eye-to-eye. "I can't get into it now, Wrenie, but I need you to go with Elisi. Go home, get cleaned up, and get some of that Elisi's Famous grub in you. You'll feel much better, you'll see." He stood up and pointed his finger at both of them. "But you better save some for me." He patted Wren's shoulder, then turned to Elisi. "I'll need the clothes she's wearing, so don't wash them. Officer Granger will follow you home to collect them."

He nodded as if saying it was time to go. "I'll be home as soon as I can. We'll talk then."

"But what about Brantley?" Wren asked. "Can he come with us? He needs—"

Her dad shook his head. "Sorry, honey. Dooley needs to run

him over to the hospital so we can make sure he's okay. And we need to get his statement. Then—"

"He didn't do anything!" Wren interrupted. "He—"

Her dad held up his hand. "We'll need a statement from you, too. Tomorrow. At the station. Now go. We'll take good care of Brantley. I promise."

Wren chewed her lip, torn between not wanting to leave Brantley and knowing it wouldn't do any good to argue. She felt Elisi tug on her arm.

Officer Granger gave them a ride to their truck so Elisi wouldn't have to walk all the way back.

Wren hit the lock button on the door the second they both were inside the truck, as if still needing protection from any other unidentified monsters hiding in plain sight.

They sat in silence, trying to process what had happened. Or maybe Elisi was waiting, giving Wren a chance to talk.

But Wren couldn't. She wanted to…but everything…stolen reports, murder boards, security videos, Brantley, the shepherd, the shovel, the blood…breaking her promise to Elisi that she wouldn't do anything dangerous…them possibly finding her mother's remains and everything *that* meant…it all collided inside her brain and made it impossible to speak. Impossible to think. Impossible to breathe.

Still, she opened her mouth to try, but it only released the floodgates.

The sobs came. She dropped her head into her hands as hard, gut-wrenching wails shook her whole body.

Elisi reached over and wrapped her in her arms.

"I—I'm—sorry—Elisi. I—I—know—I—promised." Her words came between hitched breaths.

"There, there, now," Elisi whispered in her ear. "Everything will be all right. All that matters is that you are here with me now."

Wren sunk into the comfort of Elisi's arms and her reassuring words. Her breathing slowed and her tears finally subsided. She pulled the neck of her sweatshirt up and dragged it over her face.

"Usdi, look at me," Elisi said, her face serious. "I'm sorry, too. How many times have I reminded you that we are Wolf Clan. We are protectors. You saw that poor creature in danger and acted." She sighed. "It wasn't fair for me to make you promise something that isn't your nature."

She turned the key in the ignition. "Why, you could no more stand by and do nothing than I could make your father go to a stomp dance."

For a split second they just looked at each other.

"I mean, seriously, can you imagine?" Elisi snorted. "That white man can't dance."

The image of her dad, wide-eyed, out-of-step, and TOTALLY out of his element, surrounded by Cherokee dancers, made Wren lose it. And it felt so good to laugh.

Elisi put the truck in gear and Officer Granger's cruiser fell in behind.

Chapter Thirty-Five

Wren stuck her head under the shower and watched the dirt, blood, and dog hair circle the drain. The steamy water pelted her back, as if constantly reassuring her she was safe now. It was over.

She tossed her hair back and dragged her hand down to squeegee her face. But was it? Over? Really?

Her dad said things had gotten bigger—what did that mean?

A knock interrupted her thoughts. "Usdi?" Elisi said from outside the door, "You okay, dear? Fort Gibson called, and they'd like you to leave them some hot water."

Wren turned off the knobs, pulled back the shower curtain, and wrapped herself in a towel. "Okay, okay, I'm out."

Elisi came on in, gathered Wren's soiled clothes, and put them into the paper bag Granger had given them.

"I've got you Elisi's Famous Grilled Cheese," Elisi enticed with a sing-songy tone. "And this time there's FIVE—count 'em—FIVE cheeses. Honestly, you've got to get out here—they're a thing of beauty."

Wren didn't think she was hungry, but Elisi's words made her mouth water. Suddenly, she was starving. In seconds, she was in the dining room, adorned in her usual fuzzy slippers, pajama bottoms, thermal shirt, and still-wet hair. As promised, a triangle-cut, beautifully toasted, grilled FIVE-cheese sandwich was waiting. Her shoulders relaxed. She *was* safe now. She was home.

Elisi pulled out a chair and sat down beside her, giving her time enough to eat. "Your dad called."

Wren grabbed a napkin and wiped her mouth. "Brantley? How is he?"

Elisi held up her hands. "He's fine. Just a pretty good bump on his head. And to answer your next question, his brother is fine, too. Just needed some stitches."

Wren tensed, sensing there was more. "What is it? What is it you're not telling me?"

"When they went into the garage, they found some... well... things that were disturbing. In the house, in the brother's room, they found even more."

Wren's eyes widened. "What?"

Elisi laid her hand on Wren's arm. "That poor misguided boy..." She shook her head. "They found journals, notes, things he wanted—maybe planned to do." Her voice trailed off.

Wren's hand flew to her mouth.

Elisi locked eyes with her. "Usdi...you two didn't just stop Brantley's brother from hurting animals. You may have kept him from hurting people, too."

Chapter Thirty-Six

An interview room at the police station might sound like an exciting place, but not if you're on the wrong side of the table. Wren knew she wasn't in trouble—at least she hoped not—and was just there to give her statement, but still she was nervous. She would tell the truth, of course, but, hopefully, without any collateral damage.

This room was nothing like the ones she'd seen on TV—a large room with a two-way mirror half the size of a wall that let a crowd of people on the other side spy on you. No, this room was more like a coat closet somebody had cleaned out just that morning and thrown in a table and chairs. No window. No mirror. No air. Wren tugged at the neck of her sweater. Heat, though, wasn't a problem.

"We'll be right in," her dad said as he motioned her to the table, having explained, before leaving Elisi in the lobby, that the Cherokee Marshal Service—the law enforcement agency for the Cherokee Nation—would be taking her statement, given his obvious conflict of interest. "Totally normal. Nothing to worry about," he assured them. Since Fort Gibson is located within the Cherokee Nation, the Marshals and FGPD are cross-deputized, so they frequently work together. "Just to make sure we're doing things by the book."

He put his hand on Wren's shoulder and smiled. "But I'll be right in there with you."

Wren sat on the hard plastic chair and scooched up to the table. The door closed, shutting her in as if she actually were in custody. She sighed. Last night had been restless. Tossing. Turning. Her brain swimming laps with everything that had happened, plus the not-looking-forward-to-it nervousness of today. Sleep had not been an option. She was exhausted.

She had wanted to go see Brantley this morning. Make sure he was okay—and that he didn't hate her. But her dad wouldn't let her.

"No communication—any type of communication, until I say so. This is still an active investigation." No doubt, by his tone, he meant it.

She folded her arms on the table, laid her head down, and closed her eyes.

The door cracking open jolted her awake and sent her heart racing. She hadn't realized she'd fallen asleep. For a moment, she didn't know where she was.

Marshal Stephenson, a ginormous man, made more ginormous by the police accessories he wore, entered first.

Her dad followed, filling what little was left of the room. He smiled and sat a bottled water down in front of her.

Stephenson pulled out his chair and instead, made it fly back and hit the wall like he was Superman. He shrugged sheepishly. "Sorry... thought it'd be heavier."

Her dad laughed as he sat down beside her. "Don't let this guy scare you. He's a teddy bear." He shot Stephenson a look. "A teddy bear that better know how to fix drywall."

Stephenson laughed and pulled his too-small chair back to the table. He plopped his notepad down, sat across from Wren, and smiled. She could see kindness in his eyes. The tension in her body evaporated.

"Hi, Wren, I'm Marshal Stephenson. I've heard a lot about you. Your dad is very proud."

Okay. Major throat lump. She hadn't expected that. She knew he loved her—no doubting that. But proud? Her money was betting more toward mad-to-furious for sticking her nose in police business—not following the rules.

Her eyes glistened and went to her dad.

He pulled her to him and kissed the top of her head. "Very proud."

Stephenson pulled a pen from his chest pocket, clicked it, and poised it on the yellow lined notepad. "Now, let's start from the beginning...."

She told them everything. From J.R., to being at the shelter when Landry brought in the tortured cat, searching for clues, finding Susan's video, Brantley identifying his brother..."You know, he didn't have to do that...," she made sure to add. All the way up to what had happened last night. Everything except the murder board, snooping in Landry's office, and the stolen abuse reports. Those things she kept on a need-to-know basis.

The marshal leaned forward. "We have reason to believe this individual was also responsible for the recent rash of arsons in the area. Animal abuse and arson are known precursors. Disturbed individuals trying to work up their nerve to do worse. We're lucky you found him when you did."

"Luck? No, sir." Her dad put his hand on her shoulder. "That was some right fine police work. Runs in the family."

Stephenson chuckled. "Well, you'd better watch out, Chief," he nodded toward Wren. "This one might be coming for your job."

The two men laughed as she considered the thought. Police chief? No way. Special Investigator Wren MacIntosh? Hmm... maybe.

The corners of Marshal Stephenson's smile dropped, as if he'd suddenly remembered something serious. He put down his pen, sat back, and folded his arms across his massive chest, his chair creaking under the strain. "Wren, there's one more thing I have to ask. Do you think Brantley had any knowledge of what his brother was doing?"

Chapter Thirty-Seven

The last several days had been bat-crap crazy. Wren knew Brantley wasn't involved, but Marshal Stephenson only cleared him after thoroughly reviewing his brother's journal. Unfortunately for Brantley, he was told that Steve, Brantley's pet iguana, was one of his brother's first victims.

Thankfully, Mrs. Myers had given them a pass on their presentation. "I think everything you two have done definitely qualifies as working together to leave your mark, don't you, class? I'm giving you both an A-plus-plus!" She beamed, leading the class in a rousing round of applause.

Wren's face felt hot, and she hated the attention, but, hey, if it got her out of schoolwork, so be it.

Brantley, on the other hand, stood and took a bow. "Thank you. Thank you. We'll be available for autographs in the cafeteria after class. Five bucks each."

Although Wren covered her face, she couldn't help but laugh.

It was like that everywhere. In all her classes, walking down the halls, in the girls' restroom…Kids who had never before acknowledged her existence were now vying to be her best friend. Brantley had accepted her from the beginning, defended her with M.J., confided in her about his father, and stood up against his brother. News flash...that position was already taken.

It was nice for a while, but it didn't take long before she was over it—tired of the whole thing.

Brantley met her at the bike rack. He chuckled. "Always wondered what it'd be like to be famous," he shrugged. "Guess now we know. But...you're more famous than I am, since I was, you know, unconscious most of the time."

Wren laughed and shook her head. Despite her making it perfectly clear that without Brantley none of this could've happened, there were still haters. Whispers and side-eyes thrown in his direction because of his brother. But to his credit, he paid them no attention. He scrolled right past the trolls and chose to only bask in the positive. He was amazing.

Wren backed out her bike. "Oh, hey, Dad texted me. He wants to take us all out to dinner tomorrow—our choice—for quote, 'our most excellent detective work,' unquote. You, me, Landry, Elisi, too. We can pick you up."

Brantley folded his arms and scrunched his face. "Hmm... free food...let me think..."

It started to sprinkle.

Wren zipped her jacket and pulled up her hood. "See you tomorrow," she said, pedaling off.

He yelled after her. "Have your people call...okay, see you tomorrow."

The rain continued throughout the night. Not hard. Just heavy, consistent plinks against the window glass that she found soothing. It was times like these—safe at home, warm in her bed—that she felt closest to her mom. When she could almost smell a hint of gardenias from her favorite perfume. Tonight, the air was especially thick with her spirit.

Wren's eyes filled with tears as big as the raindrops. "I hope, wherever you are, you're proud of me too, Mom."

◦❋◦

Late afternoon, the next day, Elisi patted her coat pockets and went digging through her purse. Wren knew she'd misplaced her keys again and knew exactly where they were, which Elisi knew Wren knew, but resisted asking her.

Finally, Elisi put her hands on her hips and huffed. "All right…where are they?"

Wren grinned. "Right here." And held them out in front her.

Elisi snatched them out of her hands and narrowed her eyes. "That's cheating, young lady. And it's not nice to make your poor Elisi think she's losing her mind."

"Well," Wren teased, "the good news is if you do lose it, I can find it."

"Funny. Now get in the truck before I make you walk to your hero's dinner. We're meeting your dad at the station."

The rain had stopped earlier in the day, but Fort Gibson still glistened. Brown leaves that had been roaming free had shellacked themselves to every surface.

Wren's stomach knotted the second they pulled into Brantley's driveway. The yellow police tape, still wrapped around the garage, jolted her back to that night. She hadn't expected that—hadn't expected it to still scare her after it was over.

Elisi must have noticed. She patted Wren on her leg. "It's okay," she said softly. "You're safe. Everybody's safe."

Brantley bolted out the front door and down the steps. He

195

waved and smiled a big happy-to-see you smile, apparently not bothered by living at a crime scene.

When they got to the station, they filed into her dad's office. Landry was the only one there. "Here they are!" Landry stood up from his chair. "About time…Some of us are starving. I've got a sick headache."

Wren playfully rolled her eyes.

Landry offered Elisi his chair, then he and Brantley exchanged a nod.

"Chief's still in with the mayor. He'll be here shortly."

Wren's eyes went to the wire rack of her dad's files that, for the last month, she had sorely neglected. But she knew her mom understood.

"How's Kona?" Wren asked Landry. She'd named the rescued German shepherd after her mom's favorite vacation spot, and had gone to visit him at the shelter every day.

"He's fine," Landry said. "No chip and no sign of an owner yet. You know…if nobody comes forward, we're going to have to find him a good home." He raised his brow. "Any suggestions?"

Wren turned to Elisi, her eyes dancing at the thought.

Elisi held up a hand. "Don't look at me. That's your dad's department."

A mixture of voices, coming from down the hall, grew closer. One, Wren recognized as her dad's. He rounded the corner and stepped into the office, followed by Mayor Jacobs.

Elisi started to stand. The mayor motioned her down. "No, no, sit, sit." Still, she scooted her chair around to make some space.

The mayor turned his attention to Wren and Brantley. "Well, well, well. I guess the citizens of Fort Gibson owe our two junior detectives here a big thank-you."

He turned and handed Wren's dad a credit card. "I can't very well give you a raise since you're not on the payroll." He laughed at his own joke. "But dinner is on me." He held up a hand as if expecting a protest. "No, no, I insist. Enjoy." He walked out of the office and back down the hall before anyone could even say thank you.

"Well," Wren's dad said, "that was...interesting." He held up the credit card. "So, where are we going, gang?"

Wren smiled and said, "Mexican!"

Chapter Thirty-Eight

Things had finally started to settle down and get back to normal. Not all the way back, though. For the most part, all the accolades and pats on her back that had made Wren uncomfortable were over and done with. But she did like the lingering effect of being seen—of no longer feeling like a ghost—no longer a faded part of the background.

She had to smile. She *was* proud of herself. And that was a good thing. But the better thing was knowing that it had nothing to do with how other people now saw her—and everything to do with how she now saw herself. Who knows, she could actually end up being a Cherokee badass full-time.

Cherokee BadAss. Yep, she loved it. Grabbing a red Sharpie from her backpack, she scribbled CBA across the front of her notebook. Going over and over the letters, making them as bold as could be—as bold as she wanted to be.

Their story had garnered a lot of media interest, but Wren had taken a stand. She saw this as an opportunity and refused to do any interviews unless she could also talk about her mom and MMIWG. Brantley, of course, had backed her play. Some of her classmates had even asked her if Elisi could make them a red-corded bracelet and how they could help.

Sitting in her English class, watching everyone file in, another thought creeped into her mind. For the longest time, she'd been mad at the police—at her dad, even. For the lack of information. Lack of progress. Lack of grid searches, helicopters, and candlelight vigils on her mom's behalf. The absolute last thing she had ever considered doing with her life was *anything* to do with law enforcement.

But now she was wavering. She *was* good at noticing things others miss. Good at investigating. Who knows? Maybe, one day, she could be part of a MMIWG task force and help others going through the same thing. Even if that meant she had to start one of her own.

She looked over at Brantley, sitting at his desk, head in his notebook, and thought about what she'd learned about his brother. What she'd read from the pages of his journal that had been leaked to the press. He was bullied. Bad. Mistreated. Told there was something wrong with him until he believed it.

That *was* terrible, and it made Wren feel terrible for him, but still, it was no excuse. Wren remembered back in third grade, when she started being on the receiving end of hate-filled comments and pranks and just couldn't take it anymore. She had come home crying. Never wanting to go back to school.

Elisi had taken into her into her arms and told her something she'd never forgotten. *Do not accept what they are saying, Usdi. The words of others can only hurt you if you let them in.*

So, she tried to never let M.J. get to her. She'd take a deep breath, take Elisi's advice, and refuse to let those things get into her spirit—*well, okay, most of the time anyway.* And sure, occasionally she might mouth off a snide response to M.J., but she'd never actually done anything real about it. Never stood up for herself or tried to put a stop to it. It was time. She was Wolf Clan. A protector. And that included protecting herself too.

Wren's hand shot up.

"Yes, Wren?" Mrs. Myers said.

"Mrs. Myers, I know me and Brantley didn't have to do a presentation, but I'd still like to say something, if that's okay?"

"Brantley *and I*," Mrs. Myers said. "But of course…"

Wren got up from her chair slowly. *What's that called when something sounds like a good idea in your head, but not so much once you actually go to do it?* Mrs. Myers would know—and would gladly tell her to look it up.

Brantley shot her a quick glance as if concerned with what she might say.

Once in front of the class, it felt like a hundred eyes were staring back at her. She licked her lips and tried to swallow.

She blew out a breath. *Here goes nothing…*

"Okay, you guys have been asking us lots of questions about what happened on Halloween."

The class straightened in their chairs, as if thinking this was about to get good.

Brantley's face went pale, and she could tell he wanted to bolt—out of the room, school, town, state, and country. *It's okay*, she mouthed to him.

"But I don't want to talk about it. That whole thing—" She paused. Her eyes closed as she tried to push away thoughts of Brantley's bother and M.J. She shook her head. "I'm just *so* sick of bullies."

She opened her eyes and looked around at her classmates. "I can't be the only one." She sighed and shook her head. "We've gotta do something—say something."

She raised her hand. "I'll go first." She turned toward her teacher. "Mrs. Myers, Meagan Jacobs—M.J. is a bully. She has harassed me since the third grade. I would very much like it to stop."

Wren wasn't sure, but she swore she heard gasps.

Her eyes went to Brantley. His eyes were red.

Wren's shoulders sagged. She felt so bad for him—for everything he'd been through. Absolutely none of it his fault.

The room went silent. Mrs. Myers put a hand on Wren's shoulder and gave her an understanding smile as if she was not at all surprised.

Wren looked again across the room, searching their eyes, hoping at least one person had heard her. Hoping somebody might be encouraged not to take any more crap. From M.J. or whoever.

But even if they didn't, she had. She had stood up and finally said, *Enough.* She was proud of herself. And that, for Wren, *was* enough.

Then, slowly, Brantley raised his hand. His face was full of pain. "Mrs. Myers, my father is a bully. I would very much like it to stop."

Chapter Thirty-Nine

It's amazing how fast your life can change. In what seemed like no time at all, she'd managed to get an A-plus-plus in English (which she didn't even know was a real thing), a great best friend to do stuff with, and a hundred-pound German shepherd to keep her feet warm. Her dad had been totally on board from the get-go, thinking Kona a just reward. Plus, what better way to protect the house when he wasn't there? Always thinking like a policeman.

But Elisi, being afraid of big dogs for most of her life, had required a little more convincing. Wren needn't have worried though. Once Kona lumbered over, laid the full weight of his massive head on Elisi's lap, and looked up at her with those wise, old, golden-brown eyes, she was smitten. So much so, Wren wasn't totally sure if Kona was her dog or Elisi's.

There'd been other good things too. After she'd publicly outed M.J. as the resident bully, others came forward, sharing their tales of M.J.-related woes. Rumor had it, the school had given her a choice: suspension for two weeks and writing a personal, heartfelt apology to everyone she'd offended, or withdraw from school. Wren kept her fingers crossed for the latter.

Mr. Endicott, their school principal, had contacted Child

Protective Services and was working with Brantley and his dad. Now that the chief of police, the principal, and CPS were involved—and Brantley was no longer afraid to speak up—Mr. Sims was much less likely to lose his temper. And always-awesome Landry told Brantley if he ever needed help, or a place to stay, to call him. Then quipped, "I've always got a kennel open."

She rode past houses that weeks ago had been decorated for Halloween. Except for those few that still had their Christmas lights up from last year, all the scary stuff was already gone. Only the uncarved pumpkins, corn stalks, and hay bales remained. The transition from Halloween to Thanksgiving was always an easy one.

The day, unseasonably warm, made for a great bike ride home. The arms of her unneeded jacket tied around her waist, she zigzagged from one side of the street to the other. Most of the fallen leaves had blown away to wherever dead leaves go, but she managed to find a few piles to ride through. She smiled at the crunchy sound they made underneath her wheels, and the clear skies, but mostly from the circle of warmth inside her, radiating from the center of her chest. Not from the weather, but for the first time in a long time, she recognized this strange feeling…happiness.

She coasted toward her house and saw her dad's unmarked car in the driveway. Her feet dropped to the pavement, jolting her to a stop. It was way too early for him to be home.

The familiar vise in her stomach gripped her as she dumped her bike in the yard. Was it Elisi? Brantley? Kona? Weird how many worst-case scenarios can run through your mind between the curb and the front door. Her body went numb as she reached for the knob as if her spirit wanted to protect her from whatever was on the other side. Oh God…Was it Mom?

Wren pulled her hand back. She'd gotten so caught up in everything—in life, that, for a moment, she'd actually forgotten—shoved all thoughts of dental records, DNA, and positive identifications far behind her.

How was that even possible?

She braced herself and opened the door.

Her dad and Elisi were on the sofa, just like it had been before.

Her dad jumped up and came to her.

Wren's head swiveled back and forth. "Where's Kona?"

Her dad put his hand on her shoulder, "He's fine. He's out back enjoying himself." He brought his face down to hers. And just straight out, he said it. "Wrenie, they have the results back." Without hesitation. Or maybe he just wanted to rip the Band-Aid off for both their sakes. "I didn't let them tell me. I wanted us to be together. To hear it as a family."

Wren searched her dad's eyes. She could tell he was struggling. Unsure. And her heart broke for him. How hard it must be—hurting inside and still having to try to be strong for his daughter. She wrapped her arms around him. "I love you, Daddy."

He paused, as if she had caught him off guard. "I love you, too, Wrenie," his broken voice whispered.

They made their way to the sofa. Wren kissed Elisi's cheek and sat down beside her.

Elisi, twisting a tissue in her hand, stopped long enough to pat Wren's leg. "We can do this," she said. "Either way, we can do this." Her voice was strong. But then she turned her face away and swiped a streak of wetness from her cheek, and Wren's heart broke again. For all three of them. Wife... mother... daughter... each brought its own particular kind of pain. The best they could do—all they could do—was to be there for one another.

They sat there for what seemed like forever. Each lost in their own thoughts. Each praying for—

The phone rang.

They collectively caught their breath. Wren, unable to stay seated, stood, and nervously tried to find something to do with her hands.

Her dad glanced at the phone, looked at Wren and Elisi and nodded, then answered the call. "Yes... Yes, this is he... Hold on, I want to put you on speaker."

He sat his phone down on the coffee table. They all leaned in close.

"Okay, go ahead," her dad said.

A female voice came out of the speaker. "Yes, Chief MacIntosh, as I was saying, this is Debra Matheson with the Oklahoma State Bureau of Investigation. Although the test results won't officially be available until next week, this is a courtesy call to inform you that the remains recently found in Cherokee County are not a match for your wife, Raven MacIntosh." She paused, as if not knowing herself if this news would be considered a positive or a negative. Finally, she said the only thing she could. "I'm sorry we still don't have answers for you and your family."

Wren's legs buckled beneath her. She collapsed on the floor. Her hands flew to her mouth. Soft cries escaped Elisi as she rocked back and forth, her hand clasped tightly around the band of red silk cord around her wrist.

Her dad, after the necessary "I understand.... We appreciate that.... Thank you for calling" hung up the phone and put his head in his hands. The three of them sat there, numb, as the minutes passed, each consumed in their own world. Each deciding for themselves if this had been good news or bad. Either way, there were still unanswered questions.

Kona barked. The kind of deep, impressive bark, distinctive to a German shepherd and sharp enough to jar Wren out of the maze of thoughts in her head.

She got to her feet. "He—he's probably hungry."

Elisi stood as well. "You two may not feel like it, but we should eat, too. I'll fix something simple."

Her dad sat back in the sofa and stared at the black screen of the TV. Elisi patted him on his shoulder as if to say, *We go on,* and headed toward the kitchen.

Wren went around the back of the sofa and hooked her arm around her daddy's neck. She bent down and kissed his cheek. In some ways, she felt sorry for him most of all.

She let out a long breath and headed toward the back door. She was so thankful for Kona. For the seemingly mundane things like getting him food, filling his water bowl, brushing his never-ending-always-shedding coat. They were welcomed distractions—especially today. She opened the back door. "Hey, big guy..."

The second Kona heard Wren's voice, all interest in the squirrel he'd trapped in the tree was lost. He bounded toward her, greeting her with full face kisses and those beautiful eyes that couldn't help but make her feel better. Everything about him filled her heart. Even a wagging tail that could wipe out anything in a four-foot radius. He was the Best. Dog. Ever. Her mom would've loved him.

Maybe someday...

Dinner was quiet, too. Elisi's Famous BLTs, but nobody felt much like eating or having something to say. Maybe that was for the best. Over the years, whenever there was news her dad couldn't share, clues that didn't pan out, disappointments upon disappointments, they'd drop into crisis-management mode. No rules. Just give each other space.

Wren hugged Elisi and her dad, cleared her mostly uneaten dinner, and excused herself. Kona tagged along as she went to her room, closed the door, and sprawled out on her bed. Kona jumped up, curled at her feet, and hung his head off the edge of the bed.

She stared at the ceiling as her thoughts wrestled. She remembered the little girl at the cemetery. How, for the slightest of moments, she had longed for that same definite answer. For what others call closure. If there was such a thing. Then she remembered the dry heaves and her flat-out denial when confronted with that real possibility. But what had brought her into the now, into her future, were the tears leaving streaks across her cheeks. Tears of relief that she had her purpose back.

She couldn't answer for Elisi or her dad, but to Wren, the remains not being her mom was a good thing. And her finder feelings being right about it showed she needed to learn to trust them. It was that same familiar stirring she felt deep in her gut, telling her she was going to need them.

Tomorrow she would start back with all the computer searches, sneaking into her dad's office, and going through his files, and anything else she could think of. Only this time she'd have Brantley to help her. And that gave her another feeling she desperately wanted to trust. A feeling of hope.

She sat up as once again, the night sky drew her to the window. Her hand went to the turquoise pendant around her neck. She closed her eyes as she ran her fingers over the grooved stone and tried to remember....

She could almost see her—the same dark hair, dark eyes that stared back when Wren looked in the mirror. But it had been so long now. It was hard to make her mother's smile, her laugh, her touch, come into focus. But this time, it was a promise Wren whispered into the darkness. As if somehow the winds might carry her words away and help her make them come true.

"I will find her."

More about Missing and Murdered Indigenous Women and Girls Movement

It may go by different names: Missing and Murdered Indigenous Women and Girls (MMIWG); Missing and Murdered Indigenous Women (MMIW); Missing and Murdered Indigenous Women, Girls, and Two Spirit (MMIWG2S); Missing and Murdered Indigenous People (MMIP), but they all share a common purpose: To advocate for the end of violence against Native peoples; to bring awareness that our missing are not getting the attention they deserve; to cry out for help in finding and bringing them home. A red handprint across the mouth—like Wren wears on the cover—is a symbol of that solidarity.

For more information, you can visit these websites:

Cherokee Nation—MMIP
https://www.cherokee.org/about-the-nation/mmip

The Bureau of Indian Affairs—Missing and Murdered Indigenous People
https://www.bia.gov/service/mmu

More about Fort Gibson, Oklahoma

Located near the southwestern boundary of the Cherokee Nation, Fort Gibson, established in 1824, is the oldest town in Oklahoma and rich with history. (Something Mrs. Myers would encourage you to look up.) A real town, with a real fort, and a *really* beautiful national cemetery, Fort Gibson is a great place to visit. The streets and most of the places mentioned are real too (including the casket in the shelter's storeroom), but *ALL* the characters in this story are completely made up. (With the single exception of Landry, who is loosely based on Chris Brassfield, Fort Gibson Animal Shelter Administrator extraordinaire.)

ACKNOWLEDGMENTS

Without a doubt, God has placed the right people in my path and opened the right doors at the right time. For this, and so much more, I must first give Him thanks.

To Scott, my proofreader husband, who, without complaint, will read the same page twenty-six times when I've only changed one word—only in the end to change it back. Who has believed in me since the beginning. Who is my biggest fan. I love you dearly. I couldn't have done this without you. Really.

To Anna Myers, my writing mentor and friend, who has worked tirelessly with the sole purpose of spending as much time as possible on my front porch—oh, and teaching me how to write. Who never hesitates to share her volumes of award-winning knowledge with anyone willing to do the work. Who didn't give up on me. For your guidance and friendship, Anna, I will forever be grateful.

I'm thankful too for those in my OK/AR SCBWI writing circle, especially Linda and Barbara, who are always at the ready to read, critique, repeat.

To my editor, Della Farrell, who saw promise and made an offer on only ten pages. Who, once I regained consciousness, has kindly worked with me to teach me the publishing side of the ropes. And whose insights definitely made Wren's story much, much better. Della, I can't thank you enough for being there for me every step of the way. It has truly been a pleasure I hope to repeat.

I am grateful too for everyone at Holiday House who has touched *Find Her* with their extraordinary talents. You have blown me away. I couldn't have asked for a better team to work with. Mary Lupton, your cover art of Wren is absolutely beautiful.

To Chris Brassfield, thank you so much for your willingness to share your knowledge of Fort Gibson. Your help was invaluable. Bless you for having such a big heart for animals and the community you serve. You are surely doing God's work.

And finally, to Lawrence Panther, David Cornsilk, and my fellow Cherokee citizens and members of Cherokee Language, Culture, and History who were willing to share their knowledge with Wren and me and help us learn. To all of you, I say a heartfelt *wado*. (And just so you know, we did tell M.J. there's no such thing as a Cherokee princess, but she just rolled her eyes and walked away. She's a bad seed, that one.)